# MIDNIGHT HORROR

Look for More Terrorlands Books
by Marco Chu Kwan Ching

# TERRORLAND

# MIDNIGHT HORROR

## MARCO CHU KWAN CHING

A
**PEAR**
PAPERBACK

Cover image © Nomadsoul1 | Dreamstime.com (Royalty- Free License)

ISBN: 978-0-6486664-1-7

First printing in 2021

# PART 1

# 1

*T*ick Tock Tick Tock

It was a stormy midnight, and sheets of heavy rain hammered Alison Road in orchestrated rhythm. A howling wind screamed like a banshee. Lightning lit the graphite sky in brilliant shock of white.

Billy ducked under his quilt covers with each thunderous boom. He desperately wanted to sleep. He tried counting sheep and other sleeping tricks, but, as he expected, none of them worked for him.

Poor Billy sighed wearily.

Perhaps it is because he has astraphobia.

Perhaps he can finally go to sleep when the thunderstorm goes away.

Droplets of water streaked down the windowpanes as it continued to rain.

Billy shuddered when more thunder reverberated across the malevolent sky.

Suddenly, his bedroom window flew open, and the transparent window curtain fluttered violently under the gale. The wintry wind swirled the papers flying everywhere in the room.

Reluctantly, Billy gritted his teeth and got out of bed. The floor felt icy cold. He tiptoed over to the window to shut it. The tangle of the translucent curtain wiped his face.

*Pitter-patter, pitter-patter.*

The rain battered over Billy like a volley of bullets, wetting his pajamas. Coldness enveloped him.

*Achoo!*

Billy battled with the fierce wind. Finally, he managed to shut and lock the window. He glanced down at the empty cobbled street. The artificial yellow glow of the empty streetlamps was dim under the thunderstorm.

Mom. Dad. I don't want to be alone. When are you going to be home?

*Tick Tock, Tick Tock*

Billy glanced outside the windowpane. Raindrops raced down the window in a zig-zag path, while streaks of pure white lightning forked in the utter blackness. From the corner of his eyes, the lightning momentarily revealed an unusually tall, faceless figure in a black suit at a bus stop on the opposite side of the street, in front of a forest of tall pine trees.

Oh....no. Is...is he the legendary Slender Man everybody talks about online? Is this the Slender Man who abducted Owen and other kids?

Billy rubbed his eyes to make sure he wasn't just seeing things.

Lightning struck again, and Billy's heart almost

skipped a beat when the tall figure waved at him under the heavy rain. It sent shivers down his spines.

Whoever that may be, it is coming after him tonight…

Billy quickly dived back into his bed at the speed of light; his heart was pounding fast. He wrapped the quilt covers around his head. Gasping. Sweat was cascading down his forehead like a waterfall; his hands were trembling with fear.

Please leave me alone. I know I have seen things I'm not supposed to see, Billy squeaked and murmured to himself.

*Tick Tock, Tick Tock*

The dreadful antique clock continued to tick in the still air. Even under the thunderstorm, it sounded loud and clear.

Then there was a long moment of eerie silence.

Billy slowly lowered the quilt covers and peered at the wall.

A flash of lightning revealed something strange about the clock. It tick tock, tick tock, tick tock... and then, without pause, it slammed into reverse, *tock tick, tock tick, tock tick…*

Billy rubbed his eyes to make sure he was not just seeing things. Then, he heard something inside the room.

Something that sounded like a death rattle…

It was far away at first…then it got closer and closer…

Next, Billy felt a long strand of hair snake out like writhing tentacles. Slowly, it wrapped around his neck from behind, ensnarling him, trapping him in its clutches.

Billy was paralyzed.

Just when he was about to tilt his head, to his horror, a cluster of hair fell in disarray and pounced on him.

The next thing he heard was his scream.

## 2

*C*hoo-Choo…Choo-Choo

The metallic shriek finally heralds the arrival of our train at platform twenty-three. My brother and I woke up at five-thirty this morning to catch this train. It was delayed. We were left shivering on the platform for half an hour of numbing quiet. It was such a perfect way to start the first day of our school holiday.

Oh, hi. My name is Sophia. I am twelve. I have straight blonde hair and dark blue eyes. Skinny. Oh well, not too skinny.

My brother, Ben, is nine. He is short and obese and a game addict. Every time I see him, he has his face glued to his game machine.

"Come on, Ben, our train has come," I urged.

"Just a few more minutes. I almost beat the Dark Lord," Ben replied.

See what I mean. My brother is living in his own world.

"Ben! Put that thing away. Quick. Hop onto the train. I don't want to wait for two hours for the next train," I crossed my arm and scolded.

"Alright. Alright," Ben rolled his eyes.

We hopped onto the train and slid onto a long velour bench.

I leaned my head against the carriage window. I could see a page of yesterday's newspaper chased by the wind like a pigeon with wings fluttering. The sky was gray, and unbroken shades of white and gray carpeted the sky. It looked like the sun had given up trying to break through the curtain of clouds.

Oh well, I think it is going to be a gloomy day.

The train finally departed the station after sorting out some signaling issues. It jolted and picked up its speed, juddering past rows of beautiful two-storey Victorian terraced houses. Believe it or not, they have modest decoration.

"Ben, look! It is our house!" I exclaimed.

"Ya. Ya. Whatever. I see it every day," Ben yawned, uninterested. He was still battling that Dark Lord in the game after dying again and again. Sometimes, I wonder why my little brother can be so addicted to playing games. Like Captain America in Marvel, he can do this all day.

The carriage rocked back and forth.

I gazed around my carriage. It looked like there aren't many commuters at this time of the day. An old man at the far end of the carriage was snoring like a pig. A teenager lounged back with his feet on the seat, listening to his Airpod. But, he was given an on-the-spot penalty by a ticket inspector in uniform. Guess what? He is travelling without a valid ticket.

I gazed at the passenger display screen.

It looks like we still have six hours to go before we reach Zunwich.

I can't wait to see my grandparents. I used to live with them when I was little. I had such a pleasant childhood growing up in Zunwich, and it wasn't until primary school when I moved back to the city to stay with my parents.

I kept enjoying the scene outside.

Soon, the train lurched and entered a dark tunnel.

I kept thinking about all the sweet memories I had with my grandparents and all the childhood friends I'd made in Zunwich. They are special people. I mean real special people…just like me.

My mind was filled with a carousel of thoughts.

My eyelids fluttered.

Then I felt Ben snuggle right into me.

Soon, I, too, drifted into sleep.

## 3

I awoke to the steady patter of rain upon the carriage window. The droplets scattered the nascent beam of the afternoon sun. The familiar sound of nature resonated in my ears, the soothing melody of pasture. It was like a lullaby to me.

The warmth of the sun rays bathed on my face, and reluctantly, I rubbed my dreams away.

"Sophia, look!" Ben exclaimed. He motioned me to a band of seven colors hanging in the sky in an arc.

Oh my….. It is God's graffiti.

We looked into the distance and saw several cattle were eating grass in the pasture. A boy about Ben's age was whitewashing fences for neighbors.

A moment later, the shopping center of Zunwich came into sight. The train decelerated to a stop at the terminal.

"Finally!" I yelled. I hopped outside the carriage and did a lazy stretch, followed by Ben.

It looked like the familiar Zunwich station hasn't changed a dime. They still hadn't installed the ticket machines yet. Anyone could walk in and out of the station very easily.

We took an elevator up to the second floor of the station. My grandparents were already waiting for us with a smile on their face. Grandma Jodie wore a bright green dress, her cat eyeglasses with the golden frame, making her look heaps younger. Grandpa Kewish was wearing a bright red T-shirt and a red hat. They have not aged much, fancy as usual, except Grandpa Kewish's belly fat is growing with age.

"Grandpa Kewish! Grandma Jodie!" Ben and I waved at our grandparents happily. We rushed towards them to give them a big hug.

"Sophia, Ben, you have grown a lot taller," Grandpa Kewish appraised. "I might have to look up and talk to you in a few years' time."

"Grandpa Kewish, you haven't aged much," I smiled. "What formula is Grandma Jodie using for anti-aging?"

"Happiness," Grandpa Jodie said. "Staying happy every day is the best formula for anti-aging."

Ben's stomach growled.

"Well, I think the two of you must be hungry after a six-hour trip. Let's grab some food in the shopping center first before heading back home, shall we?" Grandpa Kewish suggested.

We hopped into Grandpa Kewish's car. It was still the same classic 1969 Ferrari Red he had since I was born. It looked vintage but robust. How it still functions today shows the car has stood the test of time.

"So, Sophia and Ben, how is life?" Grandma Jodie

asked.

"Well, life is good. I had an exciting year last year. I got into selective school!" I was excited. "Only the top pupils in the class got selected every year."

"Congratulation," my grandparents said. "I've always known you were a smart girl since you were little."

"Why is that?" I wondered.

"Do you remember how I taught you the principles of farming when you were little? You picked it up so fast that it made your nephew Nelson envy," Grandpa Kewish laughed.

"Choose the right time, break up the soil, see to its fertility and moisture, hoe early and harvest early," I remembered.

"Ben, you are so quiet at the back; what are you doing?" Grandma Jodie turned around and gave Ben a chocolate nut bar.

"Oh, it is my favorite! Thank you, Grandma Jodie," Ben had a big smile on his face.

"Ben is addicted to video games," I complained. "He has been playing six hours straight."

"No, I didn't, I took a nap on the train," Ben denied.

"Yeah. Yeah. Whatever," I teased.

Our car entered a roundabout and turned left. A moment later, we were already in the parking lot of the shopping center. To my surprise, it was very full. I guess the morning rain didn't stop people from coming out shopping.

We followed our grandparents inside the plaza shopping center. The ceiling was domed high and made of beautiful acrylic glass. There was a river of people flowing in the walkways. Spacious shops were packed on both sides of the aisles. Candy Stores. Clothing shops. Retails. Supermarkets. You name it. In the background was music to soothe.

"Cool! Video game shop!" Ben's eyes opened wide with joy when he saw the big video game sign. It was like treasure hunting for him.

"Ben. Not today. Everyone is hungry," I disapproved.

"Oh, come on, Sophia," Ben said, annoyed. "This is a once in a lifetime opportunity for me."

"Don't worry, Ben. You have the whole school holidays to explore this shop." Grandpa Kewish smiled. "If you want to, we can come here every day."

"You are a spoiled kid," I murmured to Ben.

The shopping center was bigger than I thought. We walked another ten minutes before arriving at the food court. We found ourselves a spot in a tiny corner. Then Ben and I went and grabbed everybody something just to fill our stomach.

"Hey, Sophia!" A voice from behind me called.

When I turned around, I saw my childhood friend Zack.

Zack is a lot taller than a few years back. He has short brown hair and green eyes. It is said that about two percent of people in the world has green eyes, and he is one of them. I used to have a lot of adventures with Zack, exploring haunted places. We even formed a party called the Winter Club with three other friends Billy, Stan and Irvin. Zack is like our Captain. He is brave, diligent and has a sense of humor. It is never boring with him around.

The reason we get together is that everyone in the Winter Club are special kids. I mean real special kids.

"Captain Zack! Where has the time gone?" I gave Zack a big hug.

"The legendary Sophia is back," Zack smiled and did a fist bump with me. "I thought you said you would meet up with us tomorrow over the phone. What are you doing here at this time of the day?"

"Yes. I did. In fact, I just arrived in Zunwich," I replied. "How is life, by the way?"

"Cool. School life is boring, as usual. I missed the good old days when the three of us did crazy stuff and explored different places. Ever since you left Zunwich, the Winter Club drifted apart and went our separate ways," Zack sighed.

"Don't you guys catch up without me?" I wondered.

"Sophia, Grandma is waiting," Ben shouted at me from a distance.

"I am coming soon!" I turned around and replied.

"Zack, gotta go. I will see you tomorrow at noon," I said.

Zack did a two-finger salute and walked away.

After lunch, my stomach growled. Ben did a lazy stretch before we hopped back inside the car.

"Sophia, was that your boyfriend you were talking to?" Ben teased.

"Oh Ben, shut up," I felt annoyed.

"Language, sister. Language," Ben shook his head.

"I saw you were talking happily with that boy too," Grandma Jodie joined.

"Oh…that boy. His name is Zack. He is the childhood friend I've always talked about," I explained.

"Oh...Zack. I remember him now. He is so tall now. He used to come over to our place to play with you when you were little. It is such a coincidence you met him like this today," Grandma Jodie exclaimed.

"Yes. Actually, we plan to have a reunion tomorrow. I didn't expect to see him like this too," I smiled.

A moment later, our car reached a T-junction that ended in Alison Road.

"Hey, look!" Ben cried. He motioned us to the yellow and black barricade tape around one of the terraced houses. Outside the car window, I saw a very emotional middle-aged man with a few policemen questioning him. The lady next to him burst into tears.

When Grandpa Kewish drove past them, my sight shifted to a missing-boy poster on a lamp post. I wonder who did such horrible thing. The avatar of the boy in the poster gave me the creeps.

"Bad luck. Bad luck. Kewish, turn left at the next junction, my skin crawls every time I see these posters," Grandma Jodie complained. Then she turned to us with a serious look. "Sophia, Ben, I want you to stay away from this area. This is not the first time children or teens have gone missing around here."

Ben and I nodded.

My mind was filled with the missing-boy poster. Then I looked back at the terrace house. It became smaller and smaller and then disappeared from the rear car window as Grandpa Kewish drove away.

The road stretched onward. The familiar scene of Zunwich rolled by. I saw the playground my grandparents used to take me to during weekends. I imagined my younger self-playing soccer with Grandpa Kewish when I was little. Although it happened a long time ago, I felt it happened just yesterday.

The truth is that I had a happy childhood living with my grandparents. They looked after me very well.

"Sophia, do you remember that place?" Grandpa Kewish motioned me to a pink lake up ahead.

"Of course I remember. It is the salt lake!" I exclaimed.

"Huh? Why does the lake turn pink?" Ben asked.

"The lake turns pink when its salt level is high, and the weather is warm,"
Grandpa Kewish explained. "But, of course, there are several other factors as well like the algae combinations, the outdoor and water temperatures and water depth — that also must be right for the water to turn pink."

"How long will the pink last?" Ben wondered.

"The lake started turning pink last week. It usually goes back to its normal color when the weather cools, or we get more rain," Grandpa Kewish continued.

"It is a natural wonder in Zunwich," Grandma Jodie appreciated.

We drove past the pink lake. Scraggly trees appeared on both sides of the road. We continued on for another ten minutes. A yellow bus pulled up to the bus stop on the opposite lane. A few passengers got off, and the bus pulled away, sending out puffs of black exhaust behind it.

"Sophia, if you want to go to the shopping center, you can take M91. It is very convenient. There is a bus stop right outside our house. The bus comes every half an hour," Grandma Jodie advised.

"Thank you, Grandma Jodie," I replied.

A few minutes later, we arrived outside my grandparents' house. It was a two-storey red brick veneer house with a sloping roof. There was a gnarled old tree with thick roots outside that had been there since I was little, but I don't like it at all. It bent over and covered the whole house in darkness. Dead brown leaves always blanketed the lawn. Fortunately, in the center of the lawn, my grandparents had assembled a small fountain, lined with flower edgings. Red. Pink. Orange. It made the place much more beautiful.

"Kewish, I don't like this old tree in front of my lawn, it blocks all the sunlight," Grandma Jodie complained.

"Yeah. Yeah. I will ask someone to remove it someday," Grandpa Kewish replied hastily.

"But, you have been saying this for the last twenty years," Grandma Jodie shook her head.

"Have I?" Grandpa Kewish scratched his head.

"Yes. Have a look at Sophia. She's turned twelve already," Grandma Jodie forced a bitter laugh.

Grandpa Kewish opened the front door and welcomed us in. He showed us to our rooms on the second floor. It had been a long time since I'd been back here. It still has my childhood pictures hanging on the wall.

"Grandma, I am so happy you are still keeping all my photos here," I was touched.

"Silly girl, this is your little room. You've lived here since you were a baby girl. Grandpa Kewish and I missed you when you left Zunwich. We always think about you, so we decided to leave your photos here," Grandma Jodie smiled and showed me the photos. "Look at you, little Sophia, this was when you were three back then, climbing on the red leather couch outside in the sitting room."

"I never knew that Sophia looked so chunky when she was three," Ben giggled.

"Oh, come on, Ben, you have more baby fat on your face," I stuck my tongue out.

Grandma Jodie took a dozen photo albums out from a wooden cupboard. They were all labeled in chronological order. She flipped page after page and told me stories about my childhood in Zunwich. It sure looked like the chronicle of my childhood. I am pleased that my grandparents did this for me. Perhaps it is because I am their first grandchildren.

"Jodie, perhaps we should leave Sophia and Ben to rest.

It has been a long ride," Grandpa Kewish suggested. "Besides, they will be staying here during their school holiday. There is plenty of time to catch up."

"You are right. Sophia, Ben, you must be tired. Take a shower and some rest. I made the bed for you already. The bath towels are in the cupboard," Grandma Jodie said. "I will call you for dinner later."

"See you later, Grandma Jodie."

***

The nighttime came faster than I expected. I unpacked my luggage and took a hot bath. When dinner was ready, Ben was still undecided on which bedroom to stay. He kept switching from one bedroom to another. His squeaking footsteps in the corridor really annoyed me.

"Ben, would you please stop that?" I poked my head out and complained.

"Sophia, what is the matter with you? I just want to find a room I like to stay," Ben argued.

"Well, your footsteps are annoying," I snapped. "Why don't you make up your mind?"

"Kids, dinner is ready,"

Grandma Jodie's voice interrupted us from the kitchen. Ben and I hurried downstairs to see what we could help with.

When we reached the dining room, the smell of roast chicken invaded my nose. It is Grandpa Kewish's signature dish. He showed me how he coated the chicken with olive oil and seasoned it with salt and pepper. Then he placed the Coke can into the roasting rack and pushed the chicken butt halfway down the can.

It is amazing how well Coke goes with roast chicken.

Grandpa Kewish called it the Kewish Roast Chicken.

It is just irresistible.

"Just a little bit better than KFC?" Grandpa Kewish joked.

Ben chewed a mouthful of mashed potato. Before he finished, he grabbed the biggest piece of chicken leg on the table.

"Ben, slow down. This is not a competition. Where are your table manners?" I scolded.

"It looks like Ben has a good appetite. I am pleased," Grandma Jodie smiled.

"I think he has a monster appetite," I teased. "Isn't that right, Ben?"

Ben ignored me and continued chewing.

"How are your parents, by the way?" Grandpa Kewish asked. He opened a can of ginger beer and took a gulp.

"Well, they are pretty happy to finally get rid of us and have a holiday in Canada. They have been planning this for the last two years. They told us Niagara Falls is so beautiful," I said.

Grandma Jodie stopped halfway through the dinner. She went over to the kitchen to take out some pasta but then stopped halfway to pick up the magnets that had fallen from the fridge.

"Strange, those magnets don't stick on the fridge any-more," Grandma Jodie looked confused.

"Don't worry about it. We will get some more from the newsagency next time," Grandpa Kewish replied.

"But, we just bought these a week ago… anyway." Grandma Jodie shook her head. She wore a pair of kitchen gloves, took the pasta out of the oven and served it on the plate.

Ben shoved a forkful of pasta in his mouth and shrieked in pain. "Hot! Hot!"

"Careful, it's just come out of the oven," I shook my head.

Ben downed his plate of chicken stew. It was pretty good, except he filtered all the vegetables.

Ben and I helped to do the dishes after dinner. Later on, we joined our grandparents at the red leather crouch to catch up and chat.

By the time I looked at the clock, it was already nine. My grandparents gave us a goodnight hug before they went to bed,  reminding us to sleep early. They told us that everyone in Zunwich has a habit of going to bed early.

"Everyone but me," Ben smiled as soon as our grandparents left the room.

We went back to our separate rooms and prepared to sleep.

I was twisting and turning in bed all night. To be honest, I have trouble going to sleep in a bed that's not mine.

Do you feel the same, sometimes?

I kept looking at the ceiling.

I kept thinking about the missing boy on Alison Road today. I kept thinking about that creepy poster. I really want to warn Zack about it.

I kept thinking about the chocolate brown eyes of the

boy in the poster...

I felt he was screaming for someone to help him...

My mind was filled with a carousel of thoughts.

Just when my mind was about to free-fall into a dream, a scraping sound from nowhere interrupted my sleep.

How annoying?

I sat up on my bed and rubbed my eyes to focus. The clock on the wall was showing midnight already.

It must be Ben making the noise. He must be playing video games all night next door. He must be enjoying all the freedom in the world while Mom and Dad aren't here.

Ben, what is wrong with you? Why you have to be so rebellious all the time? Why can't you be a good boy and go to bed?

Frustrated. My voice felt as dry as sandpaper. I quietly sneaked inside Ben's room next door. I had to be very careful and make sure I didn't make any noise to disturb my grandparents' sleep.

"Ben, go to sleep," I spoke quietly to my brother. But to my surprise, he was already sound asleep, snoring like a pig, half of his blankets tossed to the floor.

Miserable, I decided to go back to my room. I left a small gap in the window to let some fresh air in. I stared outside the window to enjoy the night scene. Wisps of gray cloud floated over a pale moon. The trees were whispering in the cold night gale. Their twigs were waving like skeletons. A flock of black crows flew over to a hill under the moonlight.

Then I saw something else.

I saw a graveyard, the gravestones gleaming like

crooked teeth. An eerie gray, shimmering mist was cling-
ing low to the ground.

Strange. I don't remember seeing a graveyard before
when I was little.

I vaguely saw the tombstone shift, but thought it must
be just my imagination.

I decided to hop back in my bed to get back to sleep.

The ray of diffused sliver of moonlight spilled into the
room.

My lidded eyes became heavier and heavier...

A thought lingered in my mind. I remembered when
I was four, and I had the same paranormal experience
right in this room, right where I sleep now. It happened
roughly at midnight, I was battling with myself to get to
sleep, lying in bed with my eyes closed. I didn't know
how long I was half-awake. All I knew was, I wasn't
asleep. Then, at midnight, I felt a mysterious force lift
my body from the bed...higher and higher. My limbs
felt numb. I felt my face almost touch the ceiling. When
I decided to open my eyes, I felt my body free fall. And
the next thing I know, I was lying still on the bed.

This happened multiple times when I was little.

I always wanted to know who was behind this mysterious force.

Truth be told, I think I am psychic. Sometimes, I can
see things other people can't see. I can even move small
objects when I really try to concentrate, but I never seem
to be able to execute it with people around.

When I tell my grandparents and parents about this,
they just ask me not to be silly.

That was one of the reasons why I joined Winter Club with other like-minded kids like Zack. They are psychic kids, too. It became our interest to find out more about our ability.

A loud scraping awakened me abruptly again.

It looked like the sound isn't from next door but from the ceiling.

Wait a minute. Could this be a squirrel or a raccoon living up there? Oh wait, could this be a burglary? I wonder if Ben and my grandparents heard this too?

I must go and find this out for my peace of mind.

It was already three. I took a deep breath and got off my bed. I tiptoed to my bedroom door and quietly turned the doorknob.

The long, dark corridor of the house is truly frightening at night.

I didn't know where the light switches were, so I just used my iPhone as a torch.

The creaking noises resumed.

It looked like the noise is coming from the attic...

I wonder what that noise is.

I swallowed hard. I continued until I reached the staircase. Quietly, I took one step up the stairs, then another.

And another.

My stomach was halfway out of my mouth when I heard another sound from the attic.

A wave of panic swept over me. A cold shiver ran down my back like a slithering snake.

Just when I was about to race back to my room, all of a sudden, a hand grabbed me from behind.

"Sophia?" Grandma Jodie frowned.

"I...I," I stammered. I tried to speak, but no sound came out.

"It is very late," Grandma Jodie took my hands and led me back to my room. "The house is big. The light switches are here. You might have got lost in the dark, trying to find the toilet. It is opposite the fourth room, to the left."

"Grandma Jodie, did you hear something?" I asked.

"No. I didn't hear anything," Grandma Jodie replied with a blank face.

"But I heard a scraping sound from the attic, and I thought..." I protested but was interrupted.

"Sophia, it is very late. It is time to go to bed."

\*\*\*

I woke up late the next morning. I didn't sleep well at all. My muscle ached. I looked into the medicine chest mirror in the bathroom. Dark circles welled my eyes.

I decided to have a morning shower to refresh myself.

The water felt so crisp and sharp on my skin.

When I was done, I hurried down to the kitchen to join my grandparents for breakfast.

"Good morning, Sophia. Have you been staying up, playing video games all night?" Ben teased.

"Come on, Ben. You know I don't like playing video games," I said sharply.

Ben giggled. He picked up a spoon and began to gobble his bowl of cereal hungrily.

I greeted my grandparents at breakfast. It looked like they had bought my favorite Kellogg's Frost Flakes cereal. This cereal was discontinued a few years ago, but it made a triumphant return. I love, loved Tony The Tiger, the main cartoon mascot, on the packaging and advertising. It always made my day.

"Grandma Jodie, I am sorry about what happened last night," I apologized. "I should have stayed in my room. It is just that I thought someone was breaking in, and I was worried about us."

"Oh, sweetheart, it is okay. There is no need for an apology. I understand your worries," Grandma Jodie smiled.

"Maybe it is just the wind. Maybe it is mostly because of the change in temperature and humidity," Grandpa Kewish tried to convince me. "There are always strange noises around the house; I am sure you will get used to it."

"But remember, don't go up to the attic. It is dusty. It is dark. It is a storage area. You might trip over if you are not careful," Grandma Jodie warned.

"Do we have an attic in this house? I want to see it. I want to see it," Ben went wild.

"Ben, there is another reason why you should stay away from the attic," Grandpa Kewish turned solemn.

"Why is that?" Ben asked, raising his ears up like a bunny.

"It is because Henry lives there."

6

" Wh…who is Henry?" I choked. "I thought there was only the four of us in the house."

Grandpa Kewish burst out into laughter.

"It is just a joke," Grandma Jodie giggled. "There is no one living in the attic. If there is someone, I am sure I will be charging rent."

"Sophia, you've got to relax," Ben shook his head and had another mouthful of cereal.

My face turned red like a tomato. I can't believe I fell for this trick. Maybe Ben is right. Maybe I've got to relax. Maybe I need to let go of those weird thoughts. Maybe I should pretend and convince myself that the creaking roof noise I heard last night was just the wind.

***

It was a sunny, clear afternoon. I gave Zack a call to confirm meeting up at the shopping center. I went back upstairs to pick what to wear. After trying on different styles, I decided to go with a red-and-blue sweater and faded jeans with torn knees instead.

I told my grandparents that I was going out to meet my friends. Grandma Jodie kindly showed me the bus stop on the opposite side of the street.

The bus was late. I kept looking at my iWatch and the empty lots on both sides of the road. A long, gray shadow tilted over the sidewalks.

A moment later, the bus finally came, pulling up at the curb next to me, and I eagerly hopped in. The bus was almost empty. I tried to find the electronic payment system like the city bus uses, but it seemed like the bus in Zunwich was still using the old fashioned way of tokens.

*Great!*

I searched for a token and tossed it in a box next to the driver.

Then I found a spot and slid into a window seat.

The bus lurched away from the curb, bouncing along the main road. I stared out at the passing houses and villas. A girl in carrot-color hair complained when the driver drove past her spot.

"Driver, why don't you stop just then?" the girl cried angrily.

"Because you need to press the button," the bus driver snapped back.

The bus stopped for a red light. The bus driver decided to let the girl hop off. When the light turned green again, the bus turned the corner and drove past the pink lake I saw yesterday.

A baby started crying in the back seat as the bus rocked up and down. I turned around and made a funny face to distract its attention. Its mother tried her best to cradle it back to sleep.

I stared outside the window. I had to be alert because I wasn't entirely sure where the bus stop was. I just hoped that I hadn't passed the stop already. And if I did, it was going to be a long walk.

A moment later, the logo of the shopping center came into view.

The bus exited the roundabout and eased to its final stop.

I received a text message from Zack before I got off. He said that he had some bad news for me.

# 7

Winter Club. It was a joyful moment to reunite with my friends in the club. We referred to ourselves as "*The Winter Club*" because we set it up in winter. We set up this club because we are all special people who are blessed with extranormal gifts. There are no scruples here in the club.

Stan was skinny like a noodle. He had big, round, brown eyes and huge ears, and he can hear frequencies that normal people cannot hear. Irvin is an electronic geek who looked like a nerd, even without those nerd glasses. He loved to play around with electronics and sensors, and with Stan's help, Irwin claimed that he'd built a ghost detector to detect paranormal activities. Billy, on the other hand, could read the mind of others. And Zack is our leader. He possessed the power of telekinesis. In fact, it was Zack who helped me discover that I had some sort of telepathic ability. That is why I can sometimes feel things others fail to feel.

Ever since I moved away from Zunwich, the Winter

Club had drifted apart, and we all went our separate ways in life. We do keep in touch on social media, but nothing beats meeting in person.

I waved at Stan outside the food court. He was listening to his Airpod with noise cancellation.

"Do you know I can hear you from far away?" Stan grinned at me.

"Of course, I know," I said and gave him a high five.

"How was school and everything?" Stan asked.

"Good. Actually, a bit boring without you guys," I honestly replied. "I still remember the good old days when the five of us had adventures together."

"You are right, the good old days…" Stan sighed.

"Look who's here!" Irvin and Zack called us from behind. The boys bought a McDonald's meal for each of us. It is nice to know they still remembered that I love the Fillet o' fish meal.

"Sophia, you've grown taller than the photos?" Irvin flashed me a nerdy smile.

"Exercise more. Stop spending the whole day hiding in your garage," Stan teased.

"So, are we waiting for Billy?" I asked, looking around.

There was a long moment of silence. Irvin and Stan lowered their head, waiting for Zack to speak.

"Hello?" I was confused. "Where is Billy?"

"We have some bad news," Zack sighed.

"What is it?" I frowned.

"Billy went missing," Zack said bluntly. "It was Stan who discovered it first. It happened the night before you came. I just heard about it this morning."

I was startled. The image of the missing boy poster on the lamp post came back to my mind.

What is happening in Zunwich?

"It all started when Stan detected an unnatural frequency in Zunwich a couple of days ago. He called the Winter Club to investigate the source of it. We even built a prototype sensor to detect the movement of that frequency. But then, things began to get nasty when Zunwich began to have an unnaturally high rate of missing kids. Billy tried to communicate with the abducted kids to see where they are; would he have become a victim, too," Zack explained.

"The police are clueless about it," Irwin shook his head. "All they could do is post missing kid posters on the street."

"That is why we've got to find Billy. We've got to find those missing kids," Stan insisted.

"Who do you think abducted them?" I asked.

"We don't know yet. That's why we are going to find out," Zack replied.

"Count me in."

We decided to go to our secret gathering place - Irwin's basement. It was the Winter Club's headquarters, the size of a double garage. Adjacent to the brick wall were two long benches and a few cabinets. There were electronic instruments like an oscilloscope, soldering stations and meters scattered all over the bench. A printed circuit board was clamped underneath a magnifying glass, waiting to be soldered. It looked like the workshop of an evil genius.

The boys gathered at a bench on the far end. They were busying, hanging an array of light bulbs on the brick wall.

"Are you guys trying to decorate for Christmas, or do you want to be the next Thomas Edison? Why do you need so many light bulbs?" I went over next to them.

Zack inhaled a deep breath and came over to me.

"I know it sounds crazy. We are trying to communicate with Billy using these bulbs," Stan spoke in a low voice.

"Communicate with Billy using light bulbs?" I

scratched my head.

Irwin handed some paper to each of us, which had a letter on it.

"Irwin, I thought we were supposed to use your ghost meter to find Billy? I found the frequency, don't you remember? Why did we come all the way to headquarters today to post paper on the wall?" Stan sounded disappointed.

"Sorry, I still don't get what you are trying to do. Do you mean Billy has turned into a ghost?" I frowned.

"No. I didn't say that," Irwin coughed. "In fact, he lives. Stan found a specific frequency that identifies him yesterday. It is just that we can't reach him using that frequency band anymore." Irwin explained, packing his ghost meter away.

"Someone or something has deliberately shielded that frequency from us," Zack explained. "Fortunately, Billy hinted to Irwin through the flickering light bulb in his room. That is why we know he is still here somewhere... with us...in another form."

Zack looked around the empty air as if someone really existed. It sent shivers down my spine.

"If Billy is really here with us, then why doesn't he just show himself?" Stan sighed. He cupped his mouth and screamed Billy's name, but nothing happened.

"Stan, you didn't listen. We cannot communicate with Billy the way we normally do. That is why we are doing this today," Zack explained.

"Like?" Stan frowned.

"Like the flickering light bulb," Irwin tilted his nerdy

glasses.

"Put it simply. We asked a question, and Billy talked back with us through the flickering on the light bulbs. Billy will spell words out for us," Zack continued.

"Fingers crossed," Stan said.

The four of us spent the next few hours connecting an array of light bulbs with wires. With a combined effort, we stuck it onto the brick wall and placed each paper under each bulb. It was tedious.

"Cool, let's power it," Stan wiped the tears from his forehead. He connected the array of bulbs to the power point. All of a sudden, the room was brightly lit.

The four of us huddled together near a couch, trying to think of a question to ask Billy. I guess none of us could have imagined we would have to communicate with Billy like we are doing today.

"Billy, can you hear us?" Zack began to ask.

No reply.

"Billy? Hello," Irwin raised his tone.

The room went still and silent.

The only sound we heard was the electrical noise from those instruments on the bench.

"Don't be ridiculous. Billy has been abducted. We need to go out there and find him as soon as possible. We shouldn't be here playing this game," Stan rolled his eyes. "I think you are obsessed with doing this crazy witchcraft game."

"Stan! This is not a game," Irwin raised his voice. "I felt upset, too, when Billy went missing. I want to find him as much as everyone in this room."

"Hey, guys, cut it out!" Zack jumped in-between the two. "Billy will be very upset, seeing the two of you fighting each other."

I ignored the boys.

My eyes focused on the twenty-six light bulbs on the wall.

I kept imagining they would flicker.

I kept imagining that they would work.

I kept imagining that Billy would respond.

I really hoped this would work.

But, the cruel reality is that they didn't.

# 9

"So, how was the reunion?" Grandma Jodie asked me over the dining table.

"Well…it went pretty well. I was glad to see Zack and the others after so many years. Everyone has grown taller. They don't have that baby look on their face anymore," I replied.

"Sophia, have a look at what Grandpa Kewish bought me today!" Ben exclaimed. He waved all these new video games around me, thinking I'd be interested in them like him.

"Good on you. It looks like you will be spending the rest of the holiday indoors," I said sarcastically.

"Sophia, are you okay? Holidays are supposed to be relaxing. You do things you want to do. I don't get why you look so grumpy all day," Ben asked.

"Ben is right. What is wrong, Sophia?" Grandpa Kewish turned to me. "You don't look too well to me."

"Yes. My sister has got those sleepy panda eyes again," Ben added.

"Don't worry about me, Grandpa Kewish. I am fine. Maybe I am just a little bit too tired," I pretended. "Maybe I will take a hot shower and go straight to bed after dinner."

"Good idea. You need to rest more. Sleep early."

*** 

It was midnight again. I was lying in bed, looking at the spinning fan on the ceiling, hoping it would hypnotize me.

I couldn't go to sleep. I kept thinking about Billy. I kept thinking about the smile on his face. I kept thinking about the times the five of us were together. Today is supposed to be a happy reunion for the Winter Club.

"Billy, where are you?" I sighed.

A gust of howling wind made the window rattle.

When I sat up on the bed, the light on the ceiling flickered momentarily and went back to normal again.

"Huh?" I squinted at the light bulb.

Sophia, be reasonable. Stop imagining things. I told myself. How can it be Billy? It might just be a voltage drop or faulty wiring in the fixture or something.

Outside my bedroom window, broad-leaved shrubbery gossiped with the wind. A sudden gale sent the loose leaves on a dancing hypnotic ride.

A scraping noise from the attic interrupted my thoughts.

It was loud and clear. And I am definitely wide-awake.

It didn't sound like the wind. It sounded like something or someone is knocking from the attic…

My doorknob turned.

When I turned around, I saw Ben standing in the doorway.

"Hey Ben, it is very late, do you mind knocking? What is wrong with you?" I whispered angrily.

"Sophia, I am so scare…" Ben stammered. His whole body was shivering.

"There is nothing to be scared of. You are a big boy now. Come on, it is very late, let's go back to your room," I said and walked to my brother.

"No…I saw a very tall figure outside the house…he kept…he kept waving at me," Ben's voice came out in a choke.

"It is not possible. You must have played too many video games," I accused.

We went over to the window and looked outside.

Our eyes darted left and right to scan for the tall figure.

Under the moonlight, we saw a shimmering mist, clung low in a nearby graveyard. The twigs of the trees waved at us under the howling wind, warning us to go back to sleep. There was no tall figure anywhere.

"See, I told you that you are only imagining things," I spoke quietly. "Now, will you finally go back to sleep?"

The loud scraping noise from the attic happened again.

This time, both of us could hear it. There is definitely something inside the house.

"So…Sophia?" Ben pulled my sleeves.

The two of us tiptoed outside my bedroom. We quietly

shut the bedroom door to make sure no noise was made. I swore to myself that this time, I must find out the source of the sound. I couldn't afford to let it haunt me every night like this.

The corridor was dark and narrow, so I switched on the iPhone torch to illuminate our way. There were some photographs in golden frames on both sides of the wall. Some of them were my grandparents with my uncles. Others were just portraits of people. We walked past a cupboard. I had to be very careful not to knock down those vases on top of it.

Ben huddled behind me like a chicken the whole time. Yes. A chicken. There were a few times where he almost stepped onto my feet. If anything happened, I bet he would be the first one to run away.

My torchlight darted left and right.

We walked past a window of the corridor.

An immense storm echoed through the silent night. Outside the window, we could see lightning ripping the inky sky.

"Not another storm again," I sighed.

We reached the end of the corridor and arrived at the stairs to the attic.

"So…Sophia, shall we head up the attic in the morning instead?" Ben swallowed hard.

"No… If you are afraid, you can go back to your room. I am not forcing you to come with me," I flashed Ben a sharp gaze.

"But Grandma Jodie and Grandpa Kewish don't want us to go up there," Ben protested.

"Shhh. Keep your voice down. I suspect there is some-one in the attic. It might be dangerous if we don't find out," I explained.

Lightning jagged across the night sky. The flash was so bright that it momentarily brightened up the corridor and the stairway.

"I have a bad feeling about this," Ben shook his head but followed anyway.

We took one step upstairs.

Then another. And another.

"Ready?" I asked. "Three. Two. One."

Just when I was about to twist the handle of the door to the attic, to my surprise, it rattled violently on its own.

Our eyes opened wide in disbelief when all of a sud-den the attic door burst open, spewing wispy blue mist from within the attic.

The next thing we heard was our screams.

# PART 2

# 10

$B$illy woke up abruptly and found himself curled on his bedroom floor under a duvet. Everything in his bedroom was there, except the ambience was much darker and colder than before.

"What is happening to me?" Billy asked. He felt that mild headache come and go in a pattern. So, he decided to go downstairs to the kitchen to get some pills.

Billy hastily put some clothing on. When he walked outside his room, he found himself in an unfamiliar corridor with chipped green and white tiles on the wall. There were different rooms evenly spaced with one another. Each room had a rusty retro gate with chipped green paint. Old water pipes were running from the top. An omnipresent blue fog clung to the floor. An ash-like spore drifted through the air.

"Huh? Where am I? It doesn't look like where I live at all. Where is this place?" Billy was confused.

Billy put on his slippers and walked outside his door. The long corridor stretched like it would never end.

Billy examined his surroundings cautiously.

Since when did he live in an apartment?

He tried hard to think, but his mind went blank.

Billy pressed the doorbell of the other premises. Hopefully, someone could explain to him what was happening.

*Ding Dong.*

No reply.

Billy tried again and again, but it looked like the whole place was vacant. He continued to walk until he reached the end of the corridor. It was a hub connecting to different corridors. There were two elevators evenly spaced between one another. In-between the elevators, on the vintage wall, was a plate engraved with level forty-four.

Level forty-four? It doesn't sound like a good number? How did he end up being in an old apartment?

Billy pushed the lit button on the wall, and the silvery door slid open in front of him. He poked his head inside the elevator. It was like one large compartment with mirrors on four walls and silver handrails that went all the way around. The elevator door slid shut as soon as he stepped inside. He turned to the control panel to the right of the door; it was one long, silvery panel filled with rectangular buttons.

Billy pushed the button to the lobby. All of a sudden, the elevator hummed into life. He stepped back to the center of the elevator, his hands shoved into the pockets of his trousers. He looked at the floor number on the elevator LED indicator as the elevator continued to descend.

The light in the elevator flickered several times and made Billy startled.

"Don't panic," Billy kept convincing himself. He sucked in a deep breath until the elevator reached the lobby.

*Ding.*

The elevator door slid open.

Billy slowly poked his head out. The lobby was very dark. Hard resinous biological matter spread like fungus on the wall. Ash-like spores in the air moved in Brownian motions.

"What is this place?" Billy frowned. He walked past a flower-like orifice embedded on the wall. It triggered the release of spores in the form of mist.

Billy coughed and immediately backed away. He hurried outside the gate of the apartment. To his surprise, he ended up in the familiar town of Zunwich.

The sky was dark. The street was cold and empty. Billy walked alone in the empty cobbled street. The yellow light of the streetlamps was replaced by a blue glow.

A moment later, a seven-eleven shop popped up from a distance, the only shop that was brightly lid.

Billy exhaled a long sigh of relief.

"Thank God, there must be someone working there. Maybe they can tell me what is going on," Billy decided. He hurried inside the shop. To his surprise, there was no shopkeeper, but many children of his age. They were in school uniform, wandering aimlessly in the aisle. When they spotted Billy in pajamas, they all looked at him with a blank face.

"Can someone please tell me what this place is? Why am I here?" Billy asked.

"We are trying to find that out as well?" The other children replied with a blank face. "It is a cold and dark world out there. It is the light that led us here."

"Why are you not in school uniform?" one of the kids called Mathew asked.

"I beg your pardon?" Billy frowned. "It is the school holidays. I'm supposed to be at home sleeping,"

"So, how did you get here?" another kid named Lee questioned.

"Well…it sounds kind of silly. Nothing makes sense. I woke up and found myself curled on my bedroom floor. Actually, it wasn't quite my bedroom. I live in a house, but when I walked outside my room, I found myself in an unfamiliar corridor of an old apartment. It had chipped green and white tiles on the wall. I walked until I reached the end of the corridor. Then I took the elevator to a lobby filled with black biological matter, spreading everywhere like some type of fungus. Then I rushed outside the apartment and saw the light in this place. That is how I got here."

"It is strange that I had a similar experience too. I woke up in the Zunwich shopping center. The shops. The infrastructure. Everywhere is the same, except it is obscured by fog. There were root-like tendrils and membranes covering every surface," a kid named Joe spoke with synergy.

"It looks like something is going on with Zunwich,"

Billy agreed. "I wonder where everybody else is in town."

Suddenly, behind the curtain of fog, a girl in a worn school uniform staggered outside the seven-eleven shop. Her hair was all messy. She lowered her head, and we couldn't see her face.

"Hey, let's let her in," Lee suggested. He hurried over to the front glass door.

"Lee, wait, don't open the door yet," Joe warned.

Everyone moved to the front glass door and looked at the mysterious girl.

Billy stayed away. His intuition warned him that something was wrong. The way the girl staggered alarmed him; something wasn't right.

"Look! She is injured!" Someone among the crowd shouted.

The girl staggered closer to the glass door of the shop. *Closer and closer.*

The girl let out a long sad moan.

Everyone in the shop gasped in horror when they spotted dried bloodstains and bruises all over the girl.

When the girl tilted her head, she revealed a dislocated jaw, a torn tongue, and a large patch of her face rotted away.

# 11

Billy woke up abruptly on a patient bed in a brightly lit chamber. It had four white walls, no windows, but an old fashioned TV, broadcasting white noise. The LED on the ceiling was too luminous, and Billy had to blink several times to adjust to the brightness.

"Where am I?" Billy asked weakly. He felt his head heavy. When he reached out to touch his head, he discovered he was wearing some kind of 'mind reading' EEG headset. Standing next to him were a few scientists in white lab coats. They were busy reading the oscilloscopes and scribbling on their notepad.

"Hey, what is going on?" Billy shrieked. He tried to take off the creepy device on his head, but the scientists pinned him on the bed.

Suddenly, the door to the room sprang open. A man with an Einstein hairstyle entered the room. He seemed very relax and had both hands shoved inside his white lab coat. The nameplate on his lab coat spelled Dr. Dark.

"What is going on?" Dr. Dark asked. He snapped

his fingers and ordered the other scientists to leave the room.

Billy studied his surroundings with fright. His mind was messed up after layers of bad dreams.

"Wh...where am I now?" Billy shouted.

"Billy, you are in our Laboratory. Unfortunately, you are too young to understand the importance of the work we are doing in here," Dr. Dark grinned. He walked over to the oscilloscope to examine the readings. "Another bad dream?"

"I can't tell whether I am in a dream or not... What do you want from me?" Billy scolded. "Why did you abduct me here?"

Dr. Dark studied Billy from head to toe. It made Billy's skin crawl.

"We want you to re-enter the void," Dr. Dark said coldly. "Look at the TV. We want you to find someone for us. It is for your country. We want to eliminate a spy from China."

"I don't know what void you are talking about." Billy was reluctant to cooperate. "What void?"

The sound of thunder outside the room interrupted them. Dr. Dark gazed at the clock. It was already midnight.

"Let me out! Let me out!" Billy shouted.

Dr. Dark called a few guards to come in. He ordered them to drag Billy out of the room by force. Billy tried to resist, but the guards were too strong. Soon, the guards escorted Billy to a new room where computers and control panels were pinned to the wall. In the far back of the room was a four-meter high isolation tank filled with saltwater.

"Wh…what are you going to do to me? Let me go! Help! Papa! Mama!" Billy screamed again and again. The guards grabbed him tight and injected some psychedelic drugs into his arm.

When the injection was done, poor Billy staggered a few steps back. His mind was swirling. He swayed for a short moment and gazed angrily at Dr. Dark. Then everything began to fade. Before He could move again, he crumpled onto the ground like a puppet suddenly released from its string.

# 12

Ben and I choked in the blue mist. When the mist scattered, all of a sudden, ash-like spore lingered in my grandparents' house in the air.

"Achoo!" Ben sneezed loudly one after another. Apparently, he is allergic to the spores.

This is no good. This will definitely wake my grandparents up.

They warned us time after time to go to sleep before midnight. And I screwed up again and again.

I kept thinking about how to apologize to Grandma Jodie. On the other hand, I was wondering about those ash-like spores and the blue mist.

We waited for Grandma Jodie to come out of her room, but nothing happened. Thank God my grandparents were still sound asleep. Perhaps the thunder outside is so loud that Grandma Jodie couldn't hear Ben's sneeze.

Just as Ben and I decided to head back down before causing any more trouble, a mysterious rattling and scraping sound from the attic interrupted us.

I remember it; it's the sound that had kept me awake.

"Ben, did you hear that?" I spoke in a low voice. My eyes wandered to the attic again.

"Sophia, let's go…" Ben pulled my sleeves. His legs felt rubbery.

I ignored my brother and headed back up the stairs slowly. I could hear my heart beating. I stared up at the attic. My eyes checked the deep shadows in the corner of the attic.

"Hello? Is somebody there?" My voice trailed off. I shone my torch upstairs.

The rattling sound happened again.

I stopped on the third step to the darkroom of the attic.

My iPhone torch dimmed, then brightened again. Its thin circle darted on the wooden floor.

A blinding flash of lightning revealed something on the wall of the attic. I redirected the flashlight to it and squinted hard behind the blue mist. It was filled with cobwebs.

Ben and I dropped our mouths open in disbelief when the circle of light exposed an upside down human head with black hair and a pale face. Eight long, finger-like legs sprouted out from its head, scratching the wooden floor.

The creature snarled at us, crawling swiftly away into the shadows.

"Run!" I shouted.

Ben stood still. Paralyzed. I grabbed Ben by the arm

and raced down the stairs.

The circles of our flashlight darted left and right.

The scraping sound followed us closely from behind.

We wanted to warn our grandparents about the threat. When we were halfway to the corridor, we saw Grandma Jodie and Grandpa Kewish staggering out of their room.

"Grandma Jodie, Grandpa Kewish, get back! There is something…there is something in the –" I gasped.

Before I could finish, my grandparents turned to me slowly. A flash of lightning revealed their face twisted in terror, drooling with greenish globs…

"I…I am so hungry after midnight…" Grandma Jodie reached out at me with her skeletal hands. "I am so hungry."

# 13

My mind was blank.

I felt like a protagonist living in a nightmare.

What is happening to my grandparents? What is that creature living in the attic?

No matter what, we need to get out of this house. We need to get out of this house now!

I pulled Ben and sped downstairs. Gasping.

More scraping sounds followed us.

We rushed towards the front door of the house. My hands were shaking. Our light circles bounced up and down on the wooden floor. Under the silvery moonlight, we saw those human heads with long digits, crawling back and forth on the wall of the sitting room.

I know what they are trying to do. They plan to seal our exit.

"What on Earth? How come there are too many of them all of a sudden!" Ben had a horrible sneer on his face.

"They must have come from the attic. Quick. Go

through the backdoor in the kitchen!" I exclaimed. I dragged Ben to the kitchen area. It was all messy. Running water was overflowing from the kitchen sink. The fridge was left half open. Squashed tomatoes and fruits were littered everywhere on the floor.

Half way through the kitchen, we saw a human head spider was busy scrambling for leftover food in the garbage bin.

*Yuck!*

We covered our mouths in horror and disgust. I turned my flashlight off from my iPhone and sneaked past it as quietly as possible.

Suddenly, I felt a strand of hair touch me from above.

When I tilted my head, I saw the wicked face of a woman snarling at me upside down. Her broken teeth were blackened and yellow. Long digits around her head were dancing rapidly on the ceiling. I uttered a high-pitched scream when the creature leaped towards me, its long digits wrapped around my head.

Ben tried to take it off my face, but the digits of the arachnid rattled furiously. It scratched him again and again.

"Take that Dead Head Spider off me! Help!" I cried.

My eyes closed. I battled the Dead Head Spider with all my strength. I was staggering back and forth, knocking down the kitchen utensils and furniture in the kitchen.

The digits tightened its grasp. They kept pulling me towards the dead head.

*Closer and closer…*

More scraping sounds moved towards the kitchen.

"Sophia, we've got to go! We've got to go now!" Ben shrieked.

I reopened my eyes again and saw the Dead Head Spider was only inches away, its head locked in a frightening expression.

Just when I was about to scream, a snake-like tendril shot right out from the Dead Head Spider's mouth into my throat!

# 14

The backdoor of the kitchen burst open.

Ben twisted his face in surprise when a few teenagers appeared at the gate. One of them had nerd glasses. He took out some kind of electromagnetic gun and blasted the Dead Head Spider away from my face.

The Winter Club?

Zack hurried over to pull the tendril right out of my throat. When he spread his fingers, he saw strands of jelly-like slim.

I choked violently, vomiting. At some point, I even struggled to breathe.

Stan and Irwin continued to blast the Dead Head Spider away.

"Are you alright?" Zack said, helping me to get back up to my feet.

"I…I guess so," I said weakly. "How did you know I was in trouble?"

"I heard you," Stan flashed me a smile. "I heard you from miles away."

I saw Grandma Jodie and Grandpa Kewish slowly staggering down the stairs. Their rotten face gave me chills.

"This must be a nightmare. What is happening to my grandparents?" I sobbed.

"They aren't your grandparents anymore. They have turned, much like my parents," Zack interrupted.

"Guys, stop talking. We need to leave," Irwin advised.

The rain had stopped. The five of us slammed the backdoor shut and hurried to the backyard. We took long strides over the tall grass, brushing away the darting, buzzing gnats along our way.

"Hey guys, you are too fast," Ben gasped, struggling to catch up.

"Look, if you want to survive, you have to keep up to our pace," Zack said sharply.

We went over to the wooden fence. To my surprise, there was a giant hole in it.

"Hey, what have you done to my grandparents' fence?" I scolded.

"Unfortunately, we cannot enter the house through the front door. So, we had no choice but to blast a hole through the fence and go through the backyard," Irwin explained.

"Irwin is right. We were all worried about you. We didn't want you to end up like Billy," Zack said. "We cannot afford to lose another Winter Club member again."

"Sophia, you should be glad they saved your life," Ben added.

"Do you guys know what is happening?" I asked.

"We are trying to find that out, too. Something is really wrong in Zunwich after midnight," Zack said. "Everyone in Zunwich has turned into those abominations."

"Everyone else but us," Irwin emphasized.

We climbed through the hole of the fence outside the house. The boys retrieved their bikes parked outside the fence.

The road was eerily quiet. Not a single car on the road. The dim yellow glow of the empty streetlamps beamed down at us. I looked at my friends. I could tell each and every one of them had a story to tell. All of a sudden, I felt we'd become a bunch of homeless kids.

I turned around and looked back at my grandparent's house. I saw that gnarled old tree was swaying at me, as if warning me to stay away from the house too.

"There is no turning back now," Zack whispered next to me.

We crossed the road to the other side, where the bus stop is. Going back to Zunwich Central will take at least a forty-five-minute drive. Walking there is next to impossible.

"Did you guys ride all the way here to save me?" I asked.

"Yes. The Winter Club always looks after its members," Zack promised.

"That is why we must find Billy," Irwin reminded.

"It had become pretty obvious to me that this is not just some random kidnapping. There is something evil in this town," Stan advised. "Maybe we really should tell the police."

"I tried to call. No one picks up. According to Google, the closest police station is a few kilometers away east from here, right next to the Pink Lake," Irwin advised. "But there is one problem."

"What kind of problem?" Zack wondered.

"There is no route. We'd have to go through the forest and then a graveyard." Irwin read from his screen.

"I don't like the idea of travelling through a grave-yard…" Ben shivered.

"Neither do we," Zack sighed. "But right now, the safest place is the police station, what say you?"

# 15

The light of the full moon bathed on our faces. The five of us ventured inside a pine forest behind the bus stop. We swept the torchlight, dancing it left and right on the forest floor. The trail led through a grassy clearing, and we had to keep an eye on the ground, careful not to trip over those raised gnarled roots.

I introduced my brother to the Winter Club. I told them that Ben is the troublemaker I always talked about.

"Sophia, are you sure about that?" Ben raised an eyebrow to disagree.

We walked past carpets of leaves on the forest floor. Twigs and dead leaves crackled under our sneakers.

Occasionally, I could hear squirrels chasing each other in the dark. Some of them got tired of it and scurried up those tall pine trees.

We ventured deeper into the dark wood.

Soft grass tickled our feet.

Overhead, a group of falcons flew away from the pine trees when they spotted us. The soft wind they left behind rattled the bony twigs.

I studied my friends. I wondered how it was possible that they managed to save me just in time when I was in trouble. It takes them a long way to ride here by bike. They must have known something was going to happen to me in advance.

"Guys, I hate to ask again. How did you know I was in trouble?" I asked.

"We told you. I heard you scream from far away," Stan replied.

"I don't buy into that. You heard me from far away. But you live near Zunwich Central, near the shopping center. Unless you tell me you and the others can teleport, you wouldn't have made it in time when I was attacked. Now, I am asking you guys again, how did you know I was in trouble? What were you guys doing out there at midnight?" I asked again.

"Sophia, you are smart. The truth is that we don't know," Zack admitted.

"We don't know why. Good question. We … we appeared near your house," Irwin joined. "We…we just appeared."

I scratched my head. Confused.

"No, wait. We didn't just appear near Sophia's house," Zack tried to remember. "We were….we were… we were still trying to communicate with Billy after Sophia left Irwin's house. We tried again and again till midnight. Finally, we got it working... then we were so tired that we fell asleep."

"Hey, guys, it looks like my paranormal meter isn't

working again," Irwin complained, trying to change the subject.

"Oh, crap… I thought you are the electronic geek," Stan said, annoyed.

"Strange, my iPhone is not working either. The screen keeps flickering," Ben joined.

"Hey, stop changing the subject. I am asking how you guys got here!" I raised my voice.

"Shhh," Zack shushed. "Did you hear that?"

Before I realized what was going on, the boys screamed and dropped their bikes onto the ground. When I turned around, I saw an unusually tall, faceless figure in a black suit stalking us from behind. He had unusually long arms and legs. He was at least ….at least ten feet tall. He wore a red tie and gray suit.

I opened my mouth to scream, but no sound came out. My feet felt rubbery.

"Come on! Sophia, let's go!" Zack came back for me. He pulled me by the arm, and we ran aimlessly in the woods.

The Slender Man trailed behind us.

"I heard about this creature on the Internet," Irwin gasped.

"What is it?"

"It is the Slender Man! Rumor says that if the Slender Man is near, it will disrupt all the electronics nearby. The creature is malevolent. It tends to stalk children over very long periods. Sometimes, it can be hours, days, and months or even years. It loves invading its victims' minds to remove one's feeling of safety. It enjoys torturing them mentally, devolving its prey slowly into madness. Victims stalked by the Slender Man will suffer memory loss…making them lose track of time and reality," Irwin explained.

"I bet this thing took Billy. Now, it's after us," Zack said.

"How does it know about us? We've never seen it before," I asked, gasping.

"You don't understand. The Slender Man will come after any children associated with those missing kids," Irwin continued.

# 16

We ran aimlessly in the wood. Gasping. Everything beside us was like flying shadows.

I thought about everything that had happened since I'd arrive in Zunwich. I thought about the disappearance of Billy, the sound in the attic, and the horror we faced in our grandparents' house.

Nothing makes any sense. Not at all.

Finally, we exited the wood. When we turned around, we couldn't see the Slender Man anymore. We rested our backs against the palm tree trunks to catch our breath.

"Dammit, we lost our bikes," Stan complained.

"You should be glad we are still alive, for now," Irwin said. "You should appreciate that."

"Do...does that mean that thing will stalk us for the rest of our life?" Ben asked and began to cry.

"Hey, relax. We are all in this together," I gave my brother a soft hug.

"I want to go home. I want to go home," Ben whined.

"We will go home first thing in the morning, alright?"
I did a pinky swear with Ben.

"Hey guys, it looks like my paranormal meter is functioning again," Irwin exclaimed.

The five of us continued down a vague, steep slope. Beside us were bare, scraggly trees poking up like skeletons. A red black spider was dangling from a tree.

The five of us huddled next to each other.  A gust of cold gale made us shiver. I zipped up my jacket and wrapped my arms around my shoulders. A moment later, we arrived at a familiar graveyard. A shimmering mist clung low to the rows of grave.s

"I've seen this graveyard outside my bedroom," I said.

The wind blew stronger,  whipping the dry, yellow leaves from the trees. They whirled in the current and settled near our sneakers.

"Guys, I have some bad news. It looks like we have to travel across the graveyard before we can reach the Pink Lake," Irwin reported, his face glued to the screen, much like my brother playing video games.

"Irwin, careful not to trip over the gravestones," Stan warned.

"Peter Hawking," Irwin bent over a grave and read the tombstone. "Drowned in lake. 2007 to 2019. He died so young…"

"Hey, we don't want to stay here reading tombstones. We've got to move," Zack warned.

We wandered through the rows of crooked tombstones, tall yellow grasses brushing against our ankles.

Irwin glanced around the tombstones. When he was trying to catch up with us, he stumbled and tumbled forward.

The tombstone creaked, toppling over him and landed on a pile of rocks. Cracked.

We hurried over to Irwin to see if he was okay.

"Troublemaker," Stan shook his head.

"Guys, have a look at the writings," Irwin tilted his nerdy glasses and read. "Disturb our rest at your own peril."

A shiver ran down my spine.

Ben shot me a worried glance.

"Disturb our rest at your own peril? That is a good one," Stan laughed. But, then, he was stopped by a howling nearby.

The howling was soft at first…but then a long, low moan nearby made my heart skip a beat.

"Guys…" I tried to speak, but my voice came out like a tiny squeak.

I saw the tombstone shift, much like what I saw from the bedroom window in my grandparents' house. More moans and groans slowly filled the graveyard.

All of a sudden, I saw a wrinkled, decayed face slowly surface from the graveyard. I almost vomited when I saw worms crawling out from the nose and mouth of the dead face.

I cried in pain when a decayed hand reached up from the ground and wrapped itself around my ankle.

"Help!" Ben shrieked in horror when more and more hands shot up from the ground, trapping him.

Zack tried to remove that hand from me, but the grip was too strong. A few more arms poked up and grabbed him by the shirt, pulling him under the graveyard.

Stan was paralyzed. He watched in terror as more and more dead rose from the grave.

"We are ambushed! Everybody…run!" Irwin shouted. When he spun around, he saw a ghoul-like figure with dark, sunken eyes, its mouth hanging open loosely. Before Irwin could react, the ghoul lunged forward and pinned him onto the ground.

*I…I am so hungry…*

"Th…this can't be happening...this can't be real," I prayed as I was pulled underground.

# 17

"*Stop!*" I shrieked.

All of a sudden, I involuntarily unleashed a powerful wave of psychic blast, reducing all ghouls to dust. Ben and my friends were shocked, their eyes wide open in disbelief.

"Wo..wow!" Ben cried in astonishment.

I was gasping hard. Exhausted. It felt like the whole world was swirling.

I staggered a few steps forward.

"Hey, Sophia, are you okay?" Zack grabbed me by my waist just in time when I was about to collapse.

"You are truly amazing. You saved our lives," Zack thanked.

"Stan is a chicken; he just stood there and did nothing while that thing pinned me onto the ground," Irwin complained.

"I….I," Stan spluttered.

"Enough. The pink lake is close. Let's go. The police need to know what is happening," Zack broke up the argument.

The five of us continued on.

I was puzzled by the power I'd unleashed just then.

Back when I was little, I knew I was a different kid.
My grandparents just thought I was a fast learner. I
could learn how to operate complex machines that adults
do. Deep in my mind, I knew I could do more. That's
how I met Zack and other psychic kids to assemble the
Winter Club. Even so, we are only limited to moving
objects, fast learning or listening to special frequencies
from far away. It is nothing like what I did just then...

"Sophia, how did you manage to do that?" Zack wondered.

"I...I don't know. I really don't," I was absorbed in
my own thoughts.

"Maybe Sophia can help us to find Billy this way!"
Irwin suggested.

"We finally have something to agree on," Stan nodded.

We followed a vague trail and exited the graveyard
through the iron-gate. After venturing a kilometer or so,
the lake breezes blew my strands of hair flying back.
I closed my eyes to the lullaby of the pink lake. The
rhythmic pounding of the waves calmed me down, con-
juring up childhood memories.

"Guys, do you remember this place?" Zack asked.

"Of course. It is where we assemble the Winter Club,"
I said.

"There were the five of us, standing right over there,"
Zack motioned to the pavilion not far from here.

"But now there are only four of us left in the Winter's Club," Stan said sadly.

Everyone looked at the horizon of the pink lake.

Dawn had come. Darkness surrendered to the color of soothing lavender. A ray of pale light beamed down from the gray sky. Slowly, we saw a silver lining in the cloud.

"Don't give up, we will find Billy," Zack assured. "We will bring him back home."

We saw a policeman patrolling near the pavilion. When he saw us, he motioned us to come over to him.

"Kids, it is only five-thirty. What are you kids doing here so early in the morning?" The policeman questioned. "You should be home in your bed."

We explained everything that happened. Unfortunately, he wasn't taking us seriously. He dismissed it as some kind of tale.

"No, it really happened. All of us saw it happen," we protested.

"I think you kids have watched too many movies. It messes up your mind. Don't ever gather on the street at night. There are bad people looking to abduct kids," the policeman warned.

"You just don't believe us," I sounded disappointed.

"Well, do you want the police to escort you back home?" The police officer offered. "Police headquarters is just right around the corner."

"No...We are fine. It is morning already," Ben quickly replied. "We know our way."

"Teenagers nowadays…" the policeman shook his

head and then resumed his patrol.

The five of us looked at each other. It looks like going to the police station isn't such a good idea. They will escort us home and dismiss us as rebellious kids.

We walked along the lake, thinking about the midnight horror we had, thinking about how to find our friend.

Then we bumped into a middle-aged man in a gray suit and blue tie. The man had an Einstein hairstyle and pale brown eyes, which peered out from his wrinkly face.

"Kids, you look troubled," the man said. "Is there anything I can help you with?"

"Don't worry, no one is going to trust us anyway," I sounded disappointed. "Even the police think we are making up stories."

"How do you know I won't trust you if you don't tell me what is going on?"

# 18

The man introduced himself as Dr. Dark. He told us that he worked for the government. We told Dr. Dark everything we had experienced after midnight. To our surprise, he believed every word we said. He was aware of the paranormal events happening in Zunwich.

"The cases of missing kids are under our radar. The government officials are trying to find them too, but for us to find your friend, I will need your cooperation," Dr. Dark said.

"We will do everything you want if we can find our friend," Zack assured.

"Very good. For now, all of you must be very tired. Why don't you come to the government facility to have some rest first, and we will plan our next step?" Dr. Dark offered.

***

We followed Dr. Dark into a business park near the pink lake. There were so many commercial buildings inside it. We stopped in front of a multi-storey white-shingled building. The building was very long, with a row of small, square windows along its sides.

"Welcome to the Department of Energy," Dr. Dark smiled.

"The Department of Energy?" I was a bit shocked.

"The Department of Energy has a very big hierarchy. We are just a small subdivision under its umbrella. Some division is responsible for electricity transmission infrastructure, while another division focuses on emission reductions. Other divisions focus on energy policy, energy data, energy security, and the list goes on and on. We are a special division, focusing on energy research. But we control several other subsidiaries as well," Dr. Gray introduced.

We followed Dr. Dark inside the building. The walls were all white. We walked past a long, clean corridor and arrived at a guest waiting room. There was a big couch against the wall and a round table with some science magazines on it.

"Kids, you look exhausted. Do you want to take some rest?" Dr. Dark offered. He prepared some tea for us to warm ourselves up.

"Yes. Of course. We haven't slept for the whole night. Do you have beds in here?" Ben wondered.

"Sure, we have beds. We have lots of them. It is always good to take a nap if we work too hard," Dr. Dark joked. "You know…it helps to rejuvenate our mind."

"I guess we don't need to fight for the beds then," Stan said.

"No. I will give you a room each for your privacy," Dr. Dark assured. "Now, let me find the keys first. Stay here. The couch is comfortable. You can take a nap if you wish."

We thanked Dr. Dark for his hospitality.

I looked around the guest room. I felt glad that finally, someone would believe our crazy story. I wondered why the government didn't do something about it if they already knew what was happening?

Zack and the others rested on the couch, eyes closed. Within seconds, Ben was already snoring like a pig.

Well, I couldn't blame him, though. We hadn't slept for many hours and were exhausted after what we'd gone through. Perhaps we could finally rest in this sanctuary.

I tried to take a nap, but Ben's snoring was just too loud. I grabbed the magazine from the desk and flipped a few pages; hopefully, this would put me to sleep. I saw pioneer articles related to mind reading, dream sharing and new psychedelic drugs. I couldn't understand most of them because they were very technical.

I kept reading and reading...

My eyelids felt heavy, and the world turned foggy.

My head jolted down involuntarily.

I tried to shake away the dizziness.

Then I heard footsteps from the corridor. When I raised my head, I saw a few men in lab coats coming in. One of them was holding a syringe and pointed it towards me. He pressed the plunger, and liquid sprayed out from the sharp needle head.

"Hey, what is going on?" I cried dizzily. "Oh, no…it was the tea."

The men in lab coats pinned me onto the couch.

I tried to resist, but then, I felt a slight pain on my arm.

The whole world began to swirl.

Slowly, I drifted into unconsciousness.

# PART 3

# 19

When I woke up again, I was lying on a patient bed alone. The bright light above me was blinding white. I studied my surroundings. It had four white walls, with no window, but an old fashioned TV, broadcasting white noise.

Dr. Dark was sitting right next to me. He was flipping a silver coin, again and again.

"Where am I?" I said. My head ached. It felt heavy. I raised my hand to feel my head. To my surprise, I was wearing some type of brain-machine interface helmet. Dozens of wires were dangling from the helmet. They were connected to some sophisticated oscilloscopes on a bench next to the patient bed.

"You are awake," Dr. Dark said, with a smirk on his face.

"What is going on? What have you done to my brother and my friends?" I cried angrily.

"Relax. Twenty One. I will tell you how you can find your friends," Dr. Dark spoke softly.

"Who is Twenty One? My name is Sophia," I protested.

"Sophia is just your normal name in disguise. Do you know how you can learn things a lot quicker than other kids?" Dr. Dark asked.

"Well, maybe I am blessed with a good IQ," I said.

"Twenty One, stop lying to yourself. Ever since you were born, you've known you were a special kid. You possessed psychic power, not a really high IQ. That is why you find it difficult to socialize with normal kids... until you found Zack. You formed the Winter Club to welcome other kids with psychic ability," Dr. Dark said.

"How do you know about my history?" I was shocked.

"Of course I know," Dr. Dark drank a cup of water in a glass. "I know a lot about you. Your profile is in our database. It looks like you don't know much about yourself. Want to come with me?"

*  *  *

I followed Dr. Dark along a long corridor. On both sides were white rooms evenly spaced. Inside the rooms were children with brain-machine interfaces. Some of the children were looking at TVs with white noise. Others were looking at a swinging pendulum. Their faces looked dull and blank. Each child was supervised by one or more scientists.

"I thought you worked for the Department of Energy," I asked angrily.

"Correct. I am a senior research scientist and the

84

director of Zunwich Energy Research Facility. This subsidiary is under my administration. This facility is one of several national laboratories. It grew out of the scientific endeavors and our technology war with China. Our goal is to develop mind control techniques to gain intel on our enemy," Dr. Dark explained.

"Are you saying you are training these kids for psychic ability?" I asked.

"Exactly," Dr. Dark grinned.

"Hang on a second. If my guess is right, it is you who abducted Billy and the missing kids?" I cried angrily. "Why did you do such terrible things?"

"We didn't abduct Billy. Quite the opposite, we saved his life from being abducted from those things," Dr. Dark shook his head.

"What do you mean?" I frowned.

"Those things you encountered yesterday night were manifested from an accident in here. Two years ago, when we were trying to gain intel from a Chinese spy, we put one of our most powerful subjects, Leon, into a deep sleep. During the state, we ordered the child to gain information from the spy using his psychic ability. We almost succeeded in getting the information we wanted…but then, something unexpected happened… something we think is impossible to have happened."

# 20

I listened to Dr. Dark's story. He told me how he'd attempted to exploit Leon's psychic ability to eavesdrop on a Chinese agent. But, during the mission, Leon unwittingly made inter-dimensional contact with a creature from a parallel dimension known as Another World.

"Another World?" I was confused.

"When Leon made contact, a tear in space-time was created. It cracked open a rift that bridged both worlds. According to Leon, Another World is like an alternative dimension co-existing with our world, except it is cold and dark," Dr. Dark revealed.

"Where is that rift you talk about?" I asked.

"It was right here, in this building, at the deepest level," Dr. Dark said uneasily. "Are you brave enough to do a little exploring?"

"Sure." I swallowed hard.

The corridor ended. We arrived in front of a big silvery lift. Next to it was a big room where biohazard suits were kept.

All of a sudden, I had an ominous feeling about this little exploring.

"Put this on," Dr. Dark requested. "It is part of the safety protocol."

We disappeared inside the elevator as soon as the door opened. The elevator started to hum. We rode all the way down to the deepest level. It was a very long ride. I stared ahead at the elevator door the whole time.

I kept thinking about what Dr. Dark said. Is that true? Is there another dimension that co-exists with our world?

The elevator stopped with a hard thud.

When the lift reopened again, we found ourselves in an underground complex. It was very dark. Latticework of pipes and conduits crisscrossed the ceiling. The sound of dripping water sang in my ears. At the corner of the ceiling were revolving red beacon lights. Surveillance cameras could be seen in every corner.

Ahead of us was a corridor leading to a secret laboratory.

Dr. Dark turned on his torch to illuminate the path. His circle of beam danced around the floor and wall.

While traversing the corridor, to my horror, I saw overgrown gelatinous biological matter composed of tangling vines, flesh-like membranes and flower-like orifices. I reached out my hands to touch it. It was like some kind of resinous substance, dark and strong.

"I couldn't believe the infestation took place so quickly," Dr. Dark sounded serious.

"What infestation are you talking about?" I asked.

"This biological matter comes from Another World. It spread like fungi. It grew its way out from the crack Leon created at the laboratory wall. Then it infested our laboratory and now the corridor," Dr. Dark said.

We walked past the spore cluster on the corridor ceiling. When we were close, concentrated pockets of gas were released.

"Be careful of these spores. They are toxic and dangerous. My investigation team suspects these spores could be linked to hallucinations," Dr. Dark warned.

We continued to move along the corridor. Somehow, the entire place looked alien and unreal, like some kind of nest or hive…

We tore off the flesh-like membrane that blocked the door to the laboratory. Our hands were all filled with milky white gelatinous fluid.

It was disgusting.

No wonder Dr. Dark requested that I put on the biohazard suit.

When I entered the laboratory, I couldn't believe my eyes.

The whole room was hived. The black organic material was everywhere in the room. Its architecture was similar to the combination of spider webs or warren nests. Dead plants and even the carcasses of animals were deposited as part of the building material.

*Yuck!*

At the back of the laboratory was a tall wall with huge cracks on it. Tiles and cement had collapsed. The strangest thing was the heart-like structure adhered to the crack, covered by the same secreted resin we'd seen.

It was unlike anything I had ever seen in my life.

It was beating or breathing…

# 21

I headed back upstairs with Dr. Dark. Stunned.

Everything down there in the underground laboratory looked real. But, again, it also looked unreal.

"That is the reason why I need your help," Dr. Dark said.

"Help? How can I help?" I wondered. "I am not the one who created the portal."

"Leon was the psychic kid who opened this portal. Unfortunately, he has been taken by those things, abducted somewhere behind the crack in Another World." Dr. Dark continued. "The things you saw yesterday after midnight were merely the tip of an iceberg. They will come after you night after night."

"I need to find my friends first. I cannot do this alone," I insisted.

We walked along a corridor to get back to my room. Suddenly, two scientists came to Dr. Dark breathlessly, their eyes wide open with fear.

"I am sorry, Dr. Dark. We lost it. It is here," they said.

Dr. Dark looked solemn.

"It has abducted those kids."

* * *

"Hey, Dr. Dark, what is going on?" I shouted. "What is here?"

Dr. Dark ignored me. He called for the emergency protocol. All of a sudden, the sound of a siren filled the whole building. The ambience made me feel very anxious.

I turned around and looked at the ends of the corridor. Other scientists in lab coast were busy scrambling outside the lab for the exit. They looked nervous.

Behind me, security guards in biohazard suits with guns were heading to the elevator where we'd come from.

"I thought we had the creature contained!" Dr. Dark scolded.

"Unfortunately, we do not. We must evacuate the building immediately. Or worse, we…we might have to evacuate Zunwich entirely," the scientists stammered.

"You must be kidding me," Dr. Dark looked stressed.

"No. I am not kidding you. Those spores infested the entire sewer system in Zunwich. You knew it. We cannot cover up any longer. More children will go missing," the scientists revealed. "We must abandon the Psychic Project immediately."

"No. We are not going to do that," Dr. Dark denied.

Dr. Dark turned to me and rested both hands on my shoulders.

"Sophia, I am counting on you. Your brother and friends are on the other side, in the underworld. You are the only one who can save them now," Dr. Dark pleaded.

"Tell me what I can do?" I asked. "Tell me how I can save Ben and my friends."

Dr. Dark led me back inside my room.

He ordered the two scientists to lock the door to prevent anyone else from coming in.

"I need you to go into your subconscious state. I need you to enter Another World to find your friends," Dr. Dark said.

He took out a pendulum and asked me to focus on the bob on the wire swinging back and forth.

There was something hideous about the look on the doctor's face.

Slowly, my eyelid began to feel heavy, and I drifted into sleep.

# 22

I woke up in a void, a vast, endless expanse of nothingness. A thin layer of water covered the floor.

I saw an Asian a few meters away from me. He was dressed in military uniform and was about thirty years old. The strange thing is that he didn't seem to see me. Not at all.

"Lieutenant Shen, the Americans have finally found the key to open a portal to Another World. They want to weaponize it. I have gained Dr. Dark's trust to assess the cold storage of their blueprint. The cyberwarfare should standby. I will signal you when everything is ready."

Is it true? Is it not an accident like Dr. Dark said? Is the government actually working to open a portal to Another World?

Why do they have to do such a terrible thing?

I continued to listen to the Chinese spy.

"Lieutenant Shen, everything is going smoothly. Perhaps too smoothly that I think it was intentional disinformation… Be prepared for anything. I don't want to think about the consequences if they find out my identity…"

Suddenly, everything faded away from nothingness.

I found myself inside a Seven-Eleven shop together with at least a dozen kids. They were children of my age. Most of them were wearing school uniforms. They were wandering aimlessly in the aisle.

"Hello?" I approached one of them.

But the kid ignored me. Their faces looked blank. Strange kids.

"Hello, my name is Sophia. Do you know what is going on in here?" I introduced myself.

"Sophia, do you know why you are here?" One of them called Mathew asked calmly.

"I….I am trying to save my friends," I said. "Now it is my turn to ask you, why are you here?"

"We are children of Dr. Dark. He asks us to secure this shop," a child called Joanna smiled. "He built this sanctuary for us. As long as we use our psychic power to power the light on, we are safe from the Outside World."

"People don't like us from the Outside World," another child called Lee whispered.

"Sorry, I am confuse…" I frowned.

"People from the Outside World think we are different. They isolate us. We are the abandoned kids at school. We don't have any friends," Lee elaborated. His face saddened. "Until Dr. Dark found me and said we are special kids. He introduced new friends to me…new friends like Joanna."

"Dr. Dark says as long as we gather together and focus on keeping the light on, he will be very happy. That is why all of us are wandering along the aisle," Joanna talked like a riddler. "Sophia, why don't you join us? Come. Focus. The light will be on as soon as we focus and walk along the aisle. The light can protect us from the monster outside."

I looked at the mysterious kids. Puzzled and confused.

Joanna shifted her eyes to the front door of the Seven-Eleven shop and smiled. "It looks like we have someone new joining us from the Outside World."

Suddenly, the door burst open.

A gust of breeze enveloped me.

My eyes opened wide in disbelief when I saw a newcomer in pajamas come in.

"Billy?"

# 23

"Sophia?" Billy was astonished. "I…I thought I was the only one here?"

"Do you know each other?" Joanna was puzzled.

"Of course, I have been looking for Billy. The Winter Club has been looking for you. Were you trying to give us a hint on how to find you by manipulating electricity?" I asked.

"No. It wasn't me who tried to communicate with you," Billy shook his head.

The rest of the kids looked at Billy with a blank face.

"Sophia, do you know these kids?" Billy asked.

"Like you, I just came," I replied. "So, how did you get here?"

"Well…it sounds kind of silly. Nothing makes sense. I woke up and found myself curled on my bedroom floor. Actually, it wasn't quite my bedroom. I lived in a house. But, when I walked outside my room, I found myself in an unfamiliar corridor of an old apartment. It had chipped green and white tiles on the wall. I walked until I reached the end of the corridor. Then I took the elevator to a lobby filled with black biological matter. It was spread everywhere like some type of fungus. Then I rushed outside the apartment and saw the light in this place. That is how I got here," Billy replied.

"It is strange that I had a similar experience too. I woke up in the Zunwich shopping center. The shops. The infrastructure. Everywhere is the same, except it is obscured by fog. There were root-like tendrils and membranes covering every surface," a kid named Joe spoke with synergy.

"It looks like something is going on with Zunwich," Billy agreed. "I wonder where everybody else is in town."

"Hang on a second, have I seen you before? Did we have this conversation before?" Joe was confused.

Suddenly, behind the curtain of fog, a girl in a worn school uniform staggered outside the Seven-Eleven shop. Her hair was all messy. She lowered her head, and we couldn't see her face.

"Hey, let's let her in," Lee suggested. He hurried over to the front glass door.

"Lee, wait, don't open the door! I think I know what it is. Don't open it!" Joe warned.

Everyone moved to the front glass door and looked at the mysterious girl.

Billy came over to me. The way the girl staggered alarmed him; something isn't right.

"Look! She is injured!" Someone among the crowd shouted.

The girl staggered closer to the glass door of the shop. Closer and closer.

The girl let out a long sad moan.

The light in the room began to flicker when the kids lost focus and wandered away from the aisle.

Everyone in the shop gasped in horror when they spotted dried bloodstains and bruises all over the girl.

When the girl tilted her head, she revealed a dislocated jaw, a torn tongue, and a large patch of her face rotted away.

My heart skipped a beat. The look on the ghoul girl reminded me of what my grandparents were turning into…

"Run!" I felt my adrenalin rush when the ghoul girl broke the glass door of the Seven-Eleven shop. Next, she pinned Joe onto the ground with incredible strength, her fetid breath against his face. Her jaw was drooling sticky fluid. Feasting…

Other kids tried to remove her but were either bitten or scratched.

All of a sudden, screams and terror filled the entire place.

"Go. Go through the backdoor. Now!" Joanne shouted. She led us through the exit door into a long, dark corridor.

Behind us, kids were scrambling for the exit.

Everyone was pushing through the crowd to get away.

We heard the ghoul girl chasing us from behind. Her moans and groans echoed in the dark corridor.

"Hey, Lee, don't stop. Keep going!" Joanne cried as

her peer, Lee, suddenly slowed down.

"I am sorry, Joanne…I am sorry," Lee revealed the bite mark on his forearm. His eyes had turned blood red. His face was pale white.

"No. This isn't happening….I don't allow this to happen," Joanne cried.

"Go now. Lead the others out of here. Leave before I turn," Lee spoke weakly, enduring the pain.

Billy and I kept running in the corridor.

I heard the familiar sound of a siren.

"Huh? What is going on?" I asked.

The ground began to rumble. Debris was falling from the ceiling. The sound of beeping became louder. It sounded like meters or some kind of electronic instrument.

"Oh, no…it is happening again…" Billy cried.

"What is happening?" I pursued.

"There is no time to explain. Meet me at Lab 101,"Billy urged. "Remember. Lab 101!"

Before I could speak, the whole ceiling collapsed onto us.

The next thing I saw was black.

# 24

I woke up in the same bed Dr. Dark put me into sleep. The siren was ringing non-stop in the background. The oscilloscope beside my bed was recording my brain wave signal. Every time it recorded a reading, it beeped.

My eyes searched the room for Dr. Dark, but there was no sign of him.

I kept thinking about what had happened in my dream.

Or was that really a dream? Everything felt so real, yet so unreal.

I recalled what the Chinese spy said in the void.

I remembered what he said about how Dr. Dark wants to weaponize Another World. He tricked me into finding the spy so that he can eliminate him. Then I thought about what the kids in the dream were saying. I wish it was only a bad dream...

Lab 101. I reminded myself.

I quickly got up from my bed and walked to the door.

I poked my head out and saw a team of armed soldiers making their way to the elevator.

Something really bad must be going on down there, I guessed.

When the soldiers were out of sight, I quickly sneaked into a corner. My eyes searched for room number 101.

The red light of the beacon kept revolving.

I searched one corridor after another. Finally, I found a lab with a 101 doorplate.

"Billy!" I cried happily when I saw my friend resting on the bed.

I hurried over and removed that brain-machine interface helmet on his head. I untangled the wires that connected to the oscilloscope beside his bed.

"Come on, Billy. Wake up," I urged. "You told me to find you in the dream."

I slapped Billy on the face slightly. Actually, not slightly.

Slowly, he opened his eyes like a newborn baby.

"Thank you for slapping me," Billy spoke weakly.

"Don't mention it. We are friends. I will gladly slap you again. Now, we have to find my brother and the others," I said.

"Did you guys risk your life coming here to find me?" Billy was touched.

"It is a long story. First, let's get out of here," I suggested.

"It was Dr. Dark all along. Others called him Father. He is using psychic kids like us to keep the portal to Another World open," Billy accused. "He almost drowned me in that sensory deprivation tank."

"Relax. Everything is going to be fine. We just need to get out of here and –"

Just when we were about to leave the room, we saw the display screen of the oscilloscope flicker. The electronics devices in the room, one by one, malfunctioned.

"Shhhh, it is here," Billy pulled me back just when I was about to reach for the doorknob.

When we looked through the window blinds, we vaguely saw someone walking by with a pair of very long legs.

# 25

My body was frozen as the heavy footsteps thudded in the corridor.

Next, we heard blood-chilling children scream outside the room.

I covered my mouth with both hands. Startled.

"Sophia, it is midnight already…" Billy's lip was trembling. "This thing that everyone calls the Slender Man…. It has been stalking me for many days…"

"I thought Dr. Dark told me he saved you," I was puzzled.

"Dr. Dark is lying. I…I think he and the Slender Man are in the same team. That is the only reason why I am here. Dr. Dark is calculative, manipulative and cunning. All he wants is to keep the portal to Another Dimension open," Billy accused. "It is his job."

"Are you saying this Slender Man actually works for him?" I asked in disbelief.

The heavy footsteps returned.

Billy and I gazed around the room for another exit,

but all I could see were four white walls.

"Look! The air vent," Billy motioned to the ceiling.

"Clever, Billy," I appraised.

The two of us stood on the patient bed. We removed the ceiling vent with a joint effort. I helped Billy to climb up inside the air duct first because I am taller. Then I followed him from behind.

"Come on, give me your hand," Billy grabbed me by my arm.

Just when I was halfway up, all of a sudden, the handle of the door rattled violently.

## 26

"Quick! It found us," Billy cried at the top of his lungs.

Next, the door burst open. I made it inside the rectangular air duct just in time before the Slender Man reached out for me. When I looked down from the air duct, I saw a faceless man in a suit and red tie.

It tried to extend his hand to grab us, but we'd already crawled away.

"Phew, that was close," Billy uttered a sigh of relief.

We crawled forward through the narrow air duct. The cold metal surface of the duct gave me a chill. It could barely fit one adult to crawl at a time.

We continued for a few minutes and reached a T-junction, and decided to move left.

"I bet the Slender Man won't be able to follow us from now," Billy spoke.

"But we can't hide up here forever either," I said. "This is not a sanctuary. Besides, we need to find our friends."

"True. So, what is the plan?" Billy asked.

"We will find a safe vent and exit," I suggested.

We ventured through the complicated ductwork. The duct we took sloped down into lower levels and then split off into smaller sub-ducts. We randomly picked one and crawled along, hoping to find an exit.

"This is no good. I think we are crawling down underground. And it is like a labyrinth up here," Billy said dreadfully, looking at the abyss up ahead.

"Don't lose hope. We will find a way out. Trust me," I assured.

I closed my eyes and focused hard. I could vaguely hear someone gossiping from the northwest.

"That way," I said. I motioned Billy to make a left turn, go straight, and make a left turn again.

A moment later, we saw a vent ahead of us. Shafts of blue light filtered through the vent.

"Sophia, you are a genius!" Billy appreciated. "How did you know the way?"

"Psychic power," I grinned.

We crawled towards the vent slowly, trying to stay stealthy. When I was close to the vent, my palm landed on something wet. When I spread my fingers, it was covered with a gelatinous strand substance.

Yuck.

A gust of bad odor invaded my nostrils.

When I peered through the gap of the vent, I saw a familiar laboratory with overgrown gelatinous biological matter composed of tangling vines, flesh-like membrane and flower-like orifice. At the back of the laboratory was a tall cracked wall with a heart-like structure adhered onto it…

Oh, noooo…I can't believe we crawled all the way back to the underground facility.

My eyes shifted to the center of the room when I heard a familiar voice. It belonged to a scientist with an Einstein hairstyle in a biohazard suit. There were a couple of security guards next to him in the same uniform. They were harassing an abducted kid.

# 27

"Zack, thank you for bringing me these psychic kids." Dr. Dark spoke. "If it weren't for you, it would be impossible for me to harvest so many psychic energies to keep this portal open."

"Let all these kids go!" Zack shouted.

Dr. Dark uttered an evil laugh.

"You don't understand, do you? It is too late to save your friends. They are trapped on the other side…in Another World. There is no one who can save them. Soon, Another World will expand and corrupt the world we live. First, it will be Zunwich. Next, it will be the whole world."

"I will shut this rift for good," Zack challenged.

"Unfortunately, you don't have the power to close the rift. My children in Another World will fight to keep the rift open," Dr. Dark chuckled.

"What do you mean by your children? You abducted them!" Zack roared.

"Do you still remember that Seven-Eleven shop in

your dream? It is our powerhouse. Children who are permanently trapped on the other side of the rift will die to keep the light on. Because if they don't, they are all going to die in the dream, again and again," Dr. Dark laughed.

"You are a sadist," Zack shouted angrily. "You set us up!"

A shiver slithered down my spine as I listened to the conversation between Zack and Dr. Dark.

Did Zack already know Dr. Dark's plan beforehand? Is that why he lured us to the Pink Lake? Is he conspiring with the mad scientist? No wonder he avoided my question! No wonder he avoided explaining how he'd arrived just in time to save me outside my grandparents' house!

Suddenly, I felt that things were more complicated than they appeared. It is not a coincidence that all these paranormal things happened. It is deliberate.

"I will free these kids from your evil!" Zack angered. His eyes glowed white.

"Put him down," Dr. Dark smiled.

I watched in horror when several tranquilizer rounds embedded onto Zack.

I felt Zack's psychic power slowly diminish.

He collapsed onto the floor, struggling to stay awake.

"There is no need to resist. These tranquilizer rounds can put down elephants. It is time for you to join your friends," Dr. Dark said. He ordered the security guards to drag Zack to the opening of the rift.

I couldn't stand this anymore. I was going to kick the

vent open, but Billy pulled me back.

"Don't," Billy shook his head.

"Why?" I asked.

"We will only be exposed. We can't do anything about Zack now," Billy spoke in a low voice.

The heart-like structure at the back of the laboratory opened up like a rift, several tentacles and vines emerging from the abyss. They wrapped around Zack and pulled him inside the rift.

## 28

I was stunned. Helpless.

I couldn't believe I'd let those vines drag Zack inside the rift. I felt angry with myself. The Winter Club was supposed to watch each other's backs, right?

I stared at that rift in disgust. The rift slowly closed and turned back into a beating heart.

A moment later, a security guard burst inside the room and drew everyone's attention. He was gasping hard.

"Doctor, we…we have a situation upstairs," the security guards said breathlessly.

"Report," Dr. Dark demanded.

"Those test subjects in the third level have gone missing…" the security guards said.

"What? Missing?" Dr. Dark cried in a hoarse voice. "We're supposed to feed them to the rift."

"Someone … someone took them away from their room," the security guard lowered his head and said.

"Who took them? Is it the Chinese guy?" Dr. Dark guessed.

"We don't know yet," The security guard shook his head.

"Come with me. Get back upstairs. Whoever it is, the surveillance camera must have recorded it. Find those tapes for me," Dr. Dark ordered.

I waited until Dr. Dark and the security guards had disappeared from the laboratory. Billy and I kicked open the vent and lowered ourselves down. We stayed away from that beating heart as far as possible. We feared we might end up like Zack and get dragged in.

Billy and I wandered around in the laboratory. It was dim and cold. The only lights were the flashing green and red LEDs from the control panels at the corner of the room. Tangling vines, flesh-like membranes and flower-like orifices were everywhere. I brushed away a large spider web-like thread that had stuck to my face. It felt sticky and disgusting.

"Oh no, we don't have those biohazard suits," I said regrettably.

Billy studied the laboratory from corner to corner.

"I remember these…" Billy spoke, "It is just like the lobby in my dream," Billy spoke.

I walked over to a laboratory bench on my left. The black organic material on the floor almost made me slip. I saw desktops next to some test tube racks. Beside it was large papers with scribbles and diagrams left scattered everywhere on the bench.

The scientists must have left these behind.

I randomly picked one drawing up to read under the dim light. It was showing a lot of mathematical formulas and equations that blew my mind. I decided to pick up an easier one to have a look. This one was showing the Zunwich underground sewer system and how it was connected to the Department of Energy Research.

"Hey, Billy, take a look," I motioned Billy to come over.

"I am surprised you can read it like this in the dark," Billy said. He took out his iPhone and illuminated the drawing with his torch. It was showing the infestation of the sewer system as an experiment.

"What exactly is Dr. Dark trying to do?" Bill swallowed hard.

I remember how my grandparents had turned into those abominations at midnight. I remember those Dead Head Spiders in the attic. I recalled how the Slender Man in the wood chased us.

It looks like everything is linked to the experiment Dr. Dark tried to do in this laboratory. Those things that shouldn't exist came from Another World. The mad scientist is using psychic kids like us to keep the rift to the Another World open. That beating heart on the wall was like a bridge.

# 29

The thudding sound of footsteps drew our attention to the front door of the laboratory.

When we turned around, we saw Dr. Dark and the security guards standing in the doorway.

"Kids, you think I am stupid, don't you?" Dr. Dark shook his head.

Billy and I looked at the mad scientists in disbelief.

How does he know we are here?

"We have cameras everywhere in the building. You don't have any privacy in here, not even in your dreams. Your every thought, every move, every dream is recorded by us," Dr. Dark revealed.

"Why are you so interested in us? You just want to use us to keep that monstrous rift open!" I shouted.

"No. You misunderstood. Keeping that rift open wasn't part of the plan. My real goal is to study psychic kids like you. You see, human beings use only ten percent of our brain. You are different. You can use a lot more. That's why psychic kids possess telekinesis ability to move objects, blend them or manipulate matter. The Department of Energy Research wants to learn how to improve our military to abuse this ability. The rift right over there is just a byproduct of our experiment. We never intended to open such a portal at first," Dr. Dark explained.

"Let my friends go," I urged. "Rescue them from the rift."

"I'm afraid I cannot do so," Dr. Dark laughed. "You know too much."

Dr. Dark ordered the guards to tranquilize us.

"Sorry, kids," a security guard said. He reloaded his tranquilizer and pointed it at us. "Which one of you wants to be executed first?"

The rest of the security guards laughed.

*THUD THUD THUD*

Loud footsteps from outside the laboratory had everyone puzzled.

They were far away at first, but then they drew closer and closer.

All of the computer screens on the laboratory benches began to flicker.

Dr. Dark took out his tablet to look at his surveillance app, but his screen went blank.

"What the -" the security guards dropped their mouths open when a very tall, faceless man in a suit and red tie burst into the laboratory. He towered over the rest of us.

"What is that thing?" Dr. Dark cried. "Fire! Fire at will."

Before the security guards could fire, the vines and

tentacles in the room sprang into life. In the blink of an eye, they shot out at the security guards and wrapped around their waist. Some of them were pulled to the wall, enveloped by the resin. Several security guards were lifted, hanging upside down.

"What …what are you?" Dr. Dark gritted his teeth.

The Slender Man tilted his head. Several children were standing behind it. I could see some familiar faces like Matthew, Lee and Joanna.

"Father, why are you so afraid of it? Didn't you teach us to conquer our fear?" Joanna flashed a creepy smile.

Step by step, the Slender Man walked towards the poor doctor. Several tentacle-like appendages sprouted out from behind his back.

$B$illy and I looked in disgust as the Slender Man cocooned Dr. Dark to the wall of the laboratory.

"Joanna?" I sounded confused.

"I know what you think. The Slender Man is our friend. It came to our rescue," Joanna smiled.

"The Slender Man manifests from our feelings. He lived a very lonely life. He has no friends. Others isolate him. Everyone stayed away from him because he is different. They think he is some kind of monster," Lee joined.

"But sometimes, humans can be worse than monsters," Joanna stared at Dr. Dark. "Goodbye, Father. Sweet dreams."

"Nonononono...wait," Dr. Dark cried in horror as a tentacle tore the visor of his biohazard suit and slithered into his throat. His voice turned muffled. His body slowly dissolved into the resinous biological matter of the wall, never to be seen again.

We thanked Joanna for saving us. We were pleased to

see that the other psychic kids are okay, but there were still no signs of Ben and my other friends.

The Slender Man lowered his head and looked at us.

"I...I think you ...," Billy started to speak but was interrupted by Joanna.

"Stalking? The Slender Man is not trying to stalk you. He is just trying to warn you about Another World. Unfortunately, he couldn't speak," Joanna said. "This rift is corrupting the whole town. There are other psychic kids trapped inside. We must rescue them and undo the corruption at all cost."

"But how do we stop it? What if we fail to stop these biological growths from spreading?" Billy hesitated.

"If we fail, what you experience in Another World will really become our reality. The reality and that dimension will blend together like it's already happening now. First, it is only midnight. Then, when two worldlines merge, we will see those creatures in Another World rule our day, too," Joanne explained.

Billy looked at the rift again. His stomach turned inside out.

"I...I can't do it....I want to go home," Billy lowered his head and spoke. "I miss my parents. I fear I will never see them again."

"Look, I have the same fear as you, none of us want to go inside that rift, but right now, our friends are inside. And it is up to us to save them. Do you remember the oath of the Winter Team?" I asked.

"Yes. We never abandon each other," Billy smiled. "Alright, let's do it."

"I am pleased you decided to join us," Lee smiled back. "Every ounce of psychic energy counts."

We turned to every kid in the room. There were about a dozen of them. They were the same kids I saw in my dream in that Seven-Eleven shop.

"Listen up, my friends. This is not a dream anymore. You are now free. If you choose to leave, I will not force you to come with me. After all, no one knows what resides behind that rift." Joanna said.

The kids looked at each other.

"I will go," I volunteered to step forward, followed by Billy.

"I will go too!" Lee said. He was the next to join us.

"Me too!" The rest of the crowd chanted to join.

It was a touching scene.

# 31

$M$idnight was over.

The Slender Man waved at us as it slowly disappeared into thin air.

"It looks like we are on our own from now," Joanna said. She taught Billy and me how to focus to unleash our psychic energy. Only by working together as a team would we be able to rescue our friends and close the rift.

We held our hands together in a circle, eyes closed.

I felt the furniture surrounding us was lifted in the air.

Our combined energy forced the heart to open up a large rift.

"We have to rescue everyone and exit the rift before next midnight," Joanne warned. She stretched the rift open and went in, followed by me and then the other kids. The membrane of the rift felt so wet and slimy.

We followed a long dark tunnel. Everywhere inside felt so organic. The ground was heaving up and down, almost as if the ground was breathing…

A kid slipped behind us. He landed on his hands on

the ground.

"Are you alright?" Lee reached out his hand and pulled him up, but his palm was covered with slimy ooze.

"Be careful," I warned. "We don't know what these substances are."

"Sophia is right. It is uncharted territory," Joanna agreed. "We have to keep our eyes open."

We huddled together and made our way through the long tunnel.

I studied Joanna from behind. It looked like she had someone important trapped in Another World.

"I know what you are going to ask," Joanna spoke to me.

"Huh? I begged for your pardon?" I was amused.

"I am psychic too. I can read your mind," Joanna said. "I am here for Leon. He is like a brother to me."

"Leon? Do you mean the psychic kid who opened the rift?" I remembered.

"Exactly. Leon is an orphan. He is the most powerful psychic kid. Like everyone else, he is socially withdrawn. But, unlike everybody else, Dr. Dark raised him when he was very little," Joanna explained.

"Leon couldn't speak at the beginning. He has very limited vocabulary. He was socially awkward until he met us," Lee joined.

"Don't be mistaken; Leon is actually very diligent. He can learn things very quickly," Joanna corrected.

Suddenly, I remembered the Slender Man couldn't speak too. It looked like the creature actually resembled some parts of us…

We continued until the tunnel branched out.

The abyss inside the tunnel made me shiver…

Well, I am not afraid of the tunnels. It is the fear of the unknown that frightens me.

"Joanna, can you feel where the missing kids are located?" Billy asked.

Joanna closed her eyes and tried to concentrate. She kept on concentrating…. until the image in Another World flickered in her mind. She saw something moving towards us … something crawling in the tunnel…lurking…

"Guys…stay close together," Joanne swallowed hard. Sweat was pouring down her forehead like waterfalls. "I feel there is something else in the tunnel."

## 32

The children panicked. Those who had phones turned on their torch function. Circles of lights danced randomly on the tunnel wall.

"I see nothing back here," some of the children reported.

"Neither do I," Lee spoke.

Joanna was too numb to comment at that moment.

I kept my eyes open for any movement, but I couldn't see anything as well.

The tunnel ended in a T- junction. We might have to split up to find our friends.

"Joanna, can you feel if our friends are close?" I asked.

Joanna didn't reply. She seemed to be focusing only on the wall.

"Joanna?" I tapped on her shoulder.

"Oh, I am sorry. No…I still can't sense them. This place is like a labyrinth," Joanna worried.

"Shall we split?" I suggested.

"Bad idea. We should stick together," Joanna denied.

We randomly picked left. We moved past the organ-like corridor and arrived at another section. Instead of smooth and curving, the ground became rough and rugged. Epoxy-like fluid state resin blanketed every corner of the tunnel.

I stepped on some torn clothing. When I kneeled down to have a look, I recognized it belonged to my grandparents!

My heart was beating fast. My shoulders heaved with emotion.

"What is it?" Joanna came over and asked.

"This…these torn clothing…they belong to my grandparents," I cried. "I worry about what happened to them."

"Don't worry. We will find your grandparents and get them out of here," Joanna gave me a comforting hug.

"Wait a minute. If my real grandparents are here, who are those people I met when I arrived in Zunwich?" I said.

All of a sudden, a wave of fear swept over me like a pandemic.

It looks like things are turning out very different from what I expected it to be.

The tunnel ended in a chamber. Sewage like a bad odor invaded our noses.

The air was thick. Ash-like spores in the air moved randomly.

When we moved further inside, the encrusted wall inside the chamber captured our eyes.

We took a step closer to examine the wall.

Our expressions were grim.

We saw a wall of abomination.

We saw the wall was sculpted by flesh and skin. Human arms and legs were twisted in some odd angles. Heads of victims lolled. Some of the bodies were webbed on the wall and ceiling by those translucent epoxy resin we saw. Others were mummified and hung upside down from the ceiling like insects frozen in ambers.

I covered my mouth with both hands in disbelief. Some of the children almost fainted. Billy couldn't resist the horror and vomited onto the ground.

From the corner of my eyes, I could see tentacles slithering in and out of the victims' mouths.

Joanna did a prayer.

"Achoo," someone at the back sneezed loudly and startled everyone.

All of a sudden, the wall and ceiling of the chamber came to life. A mixture of hissing, scrabbling and rattling filled the chamber.

Everyone checked the corners in the chamber. We saw shadows and silhouettes glimpsed dimly through the drifting mist.

"Save me," a familiar voice drew my attention to the wall.

When I moved closer, I saw the still-intact figure of Ben, imprisoned by the hardened resin.

"Sister…save me," Ben stared at me helplessly. His face was ghostly white. "I want to go home."

"I… I will bring you home. I promise," I began to cry.

I tried to break those resins with all my strength, but they were incredibly strong. It looked as if these resins were purposely made to trap the victims.

The ear-piercing cry from the back made me startled. When I turned my head around, a shadow of human heads leaped at the children, spider legs like digits wrapped around their faces.

Billy swirled to retreat. As he turned around, he saw several dozens of Dead Head Spiders had sealed his exit.

"Everybody run!" Joanna cried at the top of her lungs.

One by one, the psychic kids turned into prey. Screams reverberated inside the chamber.

Joanna pushed me aside just in time when a Dead Head Spider leaped at my face.

"Thank you," I said breathlessly.

Both of us tried to get back up; then we realized we were standing right at a ledge. We reattempted to get back up again, but the slimy resin on the ground caught us by surprise. We lost our balance once more and slipped into a bottomless abyss.

# 33

Joanna and I woke up lying face down on the sewer platform. The walkways, machines and pipes blended seamlessly together. It stinks. I grabbed the handrail to get back up on our feet. Below was a sewer dam. Brownish green sewage water was cascading down like a waterfall through an enormous sewer conduit.

I tilted my head to look up at the ledge. It looked like those Dead Head Spiders weren't coming after us anymore.

"It is all my fault. It is all my fault," Joanna blamed herself, grabbing her ankle in pain.

"Hey, take it easy," I comforted her. "You did nothing wrong. All you wanted is to find your missing friends."

"I have miscalculated everything….Do…do you think they will forgive me?" Joanna sobbed.

"Yes. They will," I affirmed. "Let's get out of here."

I extended my arm to give Joanna a hand, but she declined.

"I am afraid I need a little rest,' Joanna spoke in a low

voice.

I heard a familiar voice calling my name.

"Grandma?" I searched the walls and ceiling.

"Sophia…"the voice spoke my name again.

"Grandma Jodie, is that you?" I called.

I focused with my psychic energy, but there was no sign of her.

"Joanna, I will come back for you. I think I heard my grandparents somewhere," I explained.

"Be careful," Joanna nodded.

\*\*\*

I climbed up the sewer conduit. The wall of the conduit was subsumed with the bodies of the unfortunate residents of Zunwich.

"Grandma Jodie!" I cupped my mouth and screamed. Sweat swirled down my forehead, making it difficult to see.

I felt shadows slithering behind me. When I turned around to check, nothing was there.

"Grandma Jodie, Grandpa Kewish, tell me where you are," I focused.

The conduit wasn't as long as I expected. It ended in a passageway that branched out like a maze.

"Sophia…,"

The wail came again.

It led me into one passageway so narrow that I had to turn sideways to slip through it.

When I was on the other size, I was bathed with those translucent resins from head to toe.

Something grabbed my knee, and I collapsed onto the ground. It was a pair of human hands. It was Zack's hands!

"Zack!" I cried. I almost burst into tears when I saw my friend was barely human anymore. His was ensnarled in a mass of vines and tentacles. His face was pale white. The black hardened resin had imprisoned his body like it had become part of him. The memory of us in the Pink Lake flashed back in my mind. We vowed to watch each other's backs.

"Sophia, I am sorry to lure you here," Zack moaned. "I am sorry. I should have told you…"

"Stop talking," I said. I tried to pull Zack out, but he cried in pain.

"Forget about me," Zack gritted his teeth.

"Never. We are good friends, don't you remember? We're supposed to look out for each other, don't you remember?

"Dr. Dark kidnapped my brother. He forced me to expose the Winter Club and bring him more psychic kids," Zack choked. "I should have known better…Tell the Winter Club I am sorry."

"It is okay… It is okay," I soothed and touched his face.

Slowly, reluctantly, Zack was being pulled inside the wall. I grabbed his hands and tried to pull him out.

"Don't let go!" I gritted my teeth and shouted.

I watched in horror as the epoxy resin wrapped around his face.

"Let me go! Let him go!" I cried furiously.

Eventually, our grip slipped.

"Goodbye, Sophia. It was nice to have you as my friend."

# 34

I sank to my knees in despair.

"Sophia…" the weak voice of Grandma Jodie spoke again.

"Grandma?" I said, wiped my tears away. I turned to the sound and broke into a run. I kept running. I brushed away the ash-like spores in the air.

I saw more and more animal carcasses scattered on the ground.

"Hang in there, Grandma!" I came pounding into another chamber filled with control panels and electrical machines. Revolving emergency lighting was flashing a reddish glow.

Besides those, I saw a wall of faces glued to the wall. Irwin. Stan. Grandma Jodie.

A massive silhouette emerged from the ruddy mist. When I tilted my head, I saw a massive, elongated head sprout out from the ceiling of the tunnel. The head was filled with cysts and minuscule particles. It had no visible facial features, except for that drooling mouth with razor-sharp teeth. It seemed to be able to control all the tentacles and mimicked Grandma Jodie's voice…

"Sophia…" It spoke.

Then I heard someone laugh at the corner in a shadow.

To my surprise, I saw Dr. Dark. He was also ensnarled onto the wall.

"Midnight is coming again. I don't think you will live till next dawn," Dr. Dark laughed.

"You are such a monster," I accused.

"Another World is in its final stage to merge with our world. By absorbing you, we will complete that goal," Dr. Dark grinned.

## 35

Before I could react, several tentacles from the walls sprouted out and grabbed my arms and legs. I tried to break loose of the grasp, but more tentacles wrapped around me. Slowly, I was lifted up in midair.

The elongated head snarled at me.

"Sophia, do not fear us," the creature talked in the voice of a child. "Join us in another dimension. We will play together. Didn't you say you wouldn't abandon the Winter Club?"

"*Nooooooooo!*" I cried.

All of a sudden, I released a powerful blast of psychic energy that melted the tentacles and the resinous materials in the chamber. Everyone in the room was released.

My knees sagged.

The creature uttered a deafening shriek. It flexed its neck and roared.

"No. No. No. It wasn't me," Dr. Dark cried in horror when the creature snapped its jaw at him. When that massive, elongated head turned to me again and grinned, its teeth were dyed in red.

"Sophia, midnight is coming soon. You can't save them," the creature spoke in Zack's voice this time.

"You don't belong here. You don't belong to our world. Go back to your own dimension," I confronted.

"You humans let us in. And now you have to let us stay…" the creature laughed.

The tentacles were resurrected. Arachnoid legs appeared at the shadows of every corner of the chamber.

Oh no…those Dead Head Spiders…

Slowly, the elongated head extended. When it was inches from my face, its jaw opened up like a petal flower. An inner striking jaw exploded outward with a gelatinous drool.

Just when it was about to snap at me, a powerful forcefield pushed it back. When I turned around, I saw Joanna, Zack and other psychic kids. They reached out their palms. A strange flow of energy repelled the creature and the Dead Head Spiders away.

"How is this possible?" The creature cried.

Next to Joanna, a boy in a new face took a step forward.

"You wicked creature, don't you remember me?" The boy asked.

"Leon, finish it!" Joanna cried.

"Leon? I thought I had imprisoned you," the creature cried. You miscalculated.

"Sophia's psychic blast melted the prison that trapped me. I can open the portal once. Now, I am going to close it myself," Leon cried. His eyes glowed white.

"No. It is midnight soon. It is midnight soon!" The creature cried helplessly when the psychic kids united together to cut open a portal to a dimension.

The creature was outraged.

It shrieked when a massive force vacuumed it from the ceiling of the chamber, never to be seen again.

"We did it! We did it!" Everyone cheered.

When the portal closed, the tentacles, vines and all organic matter originating from Another World withered.

"Thank you, Sophia. Thank you for saving my brother. Thank you for saving us," Joanna said.

Suddenly, everything in the chamber began to change.

"Huh? What is going on?" I asked.

"We are psychic kids from another dimension, different to yours," Joanna smiled.

"Excuse me?" I raise my eyebrow.

"Everything you have experienced today and everyone you have seen don't belong to your dimension either," Joanna said. "Goodbye, Sophia. It is time for you to go back home, to your dimension."

"Wait, I don't get it," I spoke. "It doesn't make sense."

The psychic kids smiled at me and waved goodbye.

When I turned to Joanna for more information, all I could see was a blinding flash of light.

# 36

"Sophia?" A familiar voice called me.

Warm sunlight bathed on my face. My eyes lazily rolled open.

The first thing I saw was Grandma Jodie's cat eye-glasses with the golden frame. Next to her were Grandpa Kewish and Ben in a casual T-shirt.

"Sophia, are you okay? You have been sleeping for the whole day," Grandma Sophia smiled.

"Grandma…Grandpa…Ben," I sobbed. I gave them a big hug. My shoulder heaved. "I missed you. I missed you guys."

"What is the matter, darling," Grandma Jodie brushed my back with her palm. "Are you feeling well?

"No…I am fine. I just had a bad dream…I just had a very bad dream," I cried.

"It is fine now. Everything is okay," my grandparents soothed me.

"Sophia, let's have breakfast downstairs," Grandpa grinned. "Guess what. I bought more of your favorite Kellogg's Frost Flakes cereal for you."

"Thank you, Grandpa. I love, loved Tony The Tiger," I wiped my tears away.

***

I met up with the Winter Club that afternoon. We cycled back to the Pink Lake. Its stunning view was beguiling. It reminded the five of us of the Winter Club we created when we were children one summer a few years ago.

"Do you believe there are monsters in another dimension of reality?" Zack asked.

"No. Why?" Billy tilted his glasses.

"Demons. Fairy. Monsters. I think you have read too many comics," Stan rejected. "Come back to reality."

"I think Zack is taking science fiction too seriously. Even these monsters exist, what would be the motivation of creatures from another dimension coming to the fourth dimension to make mischief?" Irwin said, tilting his nerdy glasses.

"Sophia, what do you think?" Zack turned to me, hoping someone would agree with him.

But I didn't reply.

Truth be told, I could care less whether another dimension existed. I wish it didn't. I wanted to enjoy the present moment more than anything.

I moved to the lullaby of the pink lake.

I closed my eyes. The rhythmic pounding of the waves calmed me down.

I don't care whether other dimensions exist.

I just want to enjoy the present moment. I just want to live a normal life.

"Hey, let's take a photo here, shall we? I suggested.

The five of us held a pose against the railing of the lullaby, with the Pink Lake in the background.

"Okay, ready? Say Cheese."

I held my iPhone high to make sure I captured everyone on screen.

The camera clicked and flashed.

That photo became our long-lasting memory.

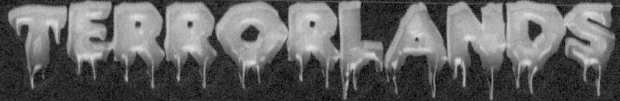

# TERRORLANDS

READER BEAWARE : YOU MAY BE IN FOR A SCARE

MARCO CHU KWAN CHING

 https://www.facebook.com/terrorlands/  https://twitter.com/terrorlands

# About the Author

Marco Chu Kwan Ching's books are read all over the world. Apart from the Terrorlands Series, Marco Chu Kwan Ching is also the author of the *Corruption of Real Money Series.*

You can learn more about his work at

www.terrorlands.com

www.corruptionofrealmoney.com

When he is not writing, he loves working on Fiverr. He has thousands of happy customers around the world.

https://www.fiverr.com/mckcvision

Marco Chu Kwan Ching lives in Australia with his wife, Carrie.

# Thank you for Reading!

*If you love my work, please feel free to leave a positive feedback on Amazon and Goodreads.*

**My contact:**
https://www.facebook.com/marco.chu.10
https://www.goodreads.com/author/show/15944678.Marco_
Chu_Kwan_Ching

**Terrorlands Facebook Page**
https://www.facebook.com/terrorlands/

**Terrorlands Twitter Page**
https://twitter.com/terrorlands

**Goodreads Page**
https://www.goodreads.com/book/show/56600560-mid-
night-horror

**Terrorlands Website**
http://www.terrorlands.com